ESCAPE THE FEAR

THE NOLA JAMES SERIES, BOOK 2

R.D. BRADY

Scottish Seoul Publishing, LLC

BOOKS BY R.D. BRADY

Hominid

The Belial Series (in order)
The Belial Stone
The Belial Library
The Belial Ring
Recruit: A Belial Series Novella
The Belial Children
The Belial Origins
The Belial Search
The Belial Guard
The Belial Warrior
The Belial Plan
The Belial Witches
The Belial War
The Belial Fall
The Belial Sacrifice

The A.L.I.V.E. Series

B.E.G.I.N.
A.L.I.V.E.
D.E.A.D.
R.I.S.E.
S.A.V.E.

The Steve Kane Series

Runs Deep
Runs Deeper

The Unwelcome Series

Protect
Seek
Proxy

The Nola James Series

Surrender the Fear
Escape the Fear

Published as Riley D. Brady

The Key of Apollo
The Curse of Hecate

Be sure to sign up for R.D.'s mailing list to be the first to hear when she has a new release!

CHAPTER ONE

NOLA

THE TOWN OF CAMERON, New Jersey, owed its existence
to the vision of Hawley Cameron Senior. Hawley Senior started
the first Cameron Canned Goods factory back in 1921, after
returning from World War I. During World War II, the factory
had been converted to manufacture munitions for the war effort.

While Hawley Junior fought in the Pacific for his country,
Hawley Senior had kept the town going, hiring war widows and
paying them the same rate as their male counterparts. Instead of
firing his war staff at the close of the war, he built a second and
then third factory, which his son helped him run.

Hawley Junior had fully taken the reins when his father
retired at the age of seventy. Both Hawley Senior and Junior,
according to all reports, had an incredible work ethic. And they
were beloved by their staff.

The apple had fallen very far from the tree when it came to Hawley Junior's son, Tommy.

Nola sat outside the Gentleman's Club at five a.m. as Tommy Cameron pushed himself out the door and stumbled onto the sidewalk. He misjudged the curb, tipping forward, but managed to keep from pitching himself face first into the parking lot.

At age forty-six, Tommy was the picture of an aging athlete. He'd played football in high school but not college. Ignoring the hundred pounds he'd gained since those glory days, he still wore athletic tanks to show off . . . something. Flabby arms? A sagging stomach? And despite the fact that the temperatures had plummeted to freezing tonight, he wore nothing over his shirt.

With the walk of a man trying to act like he hadn't had too much to drink, he made his way to his black souped-up pickup truck. Flames had been painted on the sides, and twenty-six-inch wheels had been added to allow for the six-inch lift.

Obviously Tommy was compensating for something.

Reaching the car, Tommy leaned against the wheel as he rummaged in his pockets for his keys. The brake lights blinked twice, indicating he'd achieved the milestone. It then took him two tries to reach the door handle and pull it open. Another three tries were needed before he was able to heave himself into the driver's seat.

Nola sat across the street shaking her head in disgust. Why was it the people with all the resources in the world proved to be the ones least deserving of them? At last count, Tommy boy was worth approximately five million dollars. Plus, in a few months, he would come into the lion's share of his trust, which would tack on an additional ten million.

And what did he do with his abundance? Spent it on strippers and toys for himself.

Oh, and terrorizing the illegal immigrants who worked in his factories.

Across the street, Tommy's engine flared to life. He pulled out of the spot and over the sidewalk before bouncing onto the road. He weaved his way across the yellow line so much that it was a miracle he didn't hit anyone. Halfway to his home, Nola was sure he wouldn't make it. Part of her thought it would be a good thing if he didn't. It would solve a lot of problems.

But the lucky bastard pulled into his drive without even an extra scratch on his custom paint job.

Nola pulled in across the street. Parallel lines covered the sprawling lawn of Tommy Cameron's estate. Bushes shaped like diamonds lined the long drive. The lawn maintenance crew was obviously paid a lot of money to make the place look good.

And it did.

The home stood out amongst the other large ornate mansions in the small New Jersey neighborhood. But then again, it should. It had been the first mansion in the area. Originally it had sat on twenty-six acres. Now it sat on a mere twelve. Of course, all the other McMansions were on lots no larger than two.

Nola watched as the truck's lights went out. Tommy didn't get out right away. She had no doubt he was struggling to figure out either how to unbuckle himself or how to remove the key from the ignition.

What a tool.

With a sigh, she flicked a glance at the recording equipment on the passenger seat of her Bronco. It hadn't been hard to record Tommy's activities at the strip club. The club already had a monitoring system set up to record. It took little effort for Nola to tap into the feed.

The monitoring system itself hadn't been set up to protect either the club's employees or clientele. No, the system was created to enable a healthy side business: blackmail. More than one politician, religious leader, or other pillars of the community had paid handsome sums to keep the high-definition images of their activities in the club private.

But the Gentleman's Club owner had never attempted to blackmail Tommy. With Tommy's money and clout, it would cause too many problems for too many people to risk. In fact, the strip bar owner's brother worked as a manager in one of the Hawley factories. So once again, Tommy was insulated from acts where other people would be held to account.

Across the street, Tommy finally managed to extricate himself from the driver's seat, although his foot got caught in the car door. For one happy moment, Nola pictured him plowing face first into the drive.

Alas, that happy image was not fulfilled, as he managed to free himself from his beast of a truck.

Standing on the driveway, Tommy held on to the door, swaying for a moment before he managed to close it and head toward the house. The dim light made it impossible to pick out the frosted tips Tommy had touched up every two weeks.

Nola watched him go while all that she knew about him rolled through her mind. On paper, he was squeaky clean: no tickets, no arrests, he paid his taxes, and even contributed to charity.

But none of those details provided an accurate portrait of Tommy Cameron. He'd been the late-in-life child to Hawley Junior and his deceased wife, Marjorie. And they'd spoiled the child something rotten.

And the rot had stuck.

Tommy had never married. By the grace of God, he'd never procreated either. Although that was probably less by design and more due to the heavy steroid use earlier in his life.

There was also a string of ex-girlfriends who, if they weren't scared out of their minds, would testify to his abusive nature and extravagant lifestyle.

Tommy boy was in charge of six Hawley factories in New Jersey alone, as well as the factory that had just opened up across the border in Pennsylvania. He didn't go to them every day, of course. According to Tommy, only fools had nine-to-five jobs. No, Tommy would show up at each factory once about every two weeks to check and make sure everything was fine.

And to scare the hell out of the people working there.

Because Tommy hired mainly illegals for the factory floor. He liked hiring illegals because he could put them on the payroll at the regular pay and then take half of their salary. And if anybody dared complain, he threatened to call ICE.

Amazingly, that wasn't the worst of his crimes.

Nola stepped out of her car. She quickly walked across the road. She wore black, including a ski mask and gloves. She'd already taken care of the cameras earlier. In fact, right now, lights were still on in the house, although with the flip of a switch, she would be able to take care of that. She didn't need Tommy identifying her. Not that she was overly concerned about it. He was so drunk, she wasn't sure he'd recognize himself in a mirror. But old habits die hard.

She walked over to the patio and, hopping over the short wall, wended her way around the fire pit to the side door that she'd left open for herself. She'd been in Tommy's home earlier today. It was kept immaculately clean. Apparently old Tommy was a germaphobe.

Growing up, the Cameron family had had a full-time maid who'd worked for the family for forty years. She had quit last year after Hawley Junior had moved down to Florida.

Now Tommy had two maids in their early thirties, Ava and Maria, who were both from Guatemala. They lived together in a room at the back of the kitchen. Neither one had papers and both were terrified of Tommy. They scurried around his home like mice.

Nola had spoken with them earlier. They had been terrified, but she had finally gotten them to open up about Tommy.

And then she'd gotten them the hell out of there.

If she hadn't despised him already, the tales they told her would have ensured it. Their accounts of Tommy's behavior had made her skin crawl. He'd subjected both of them to physical, sexual, and psychological abuse.

Nola picked up the bat that Tommy had displayed behind the back of his couch in his entertainment room. He was so proud of it. It was a Mickey Mantle bat from a 1953 Yankees game. Retail value: $81,000.

She took a practice swing. Yup, this would do nicely.

Nola took a right outside the entertainment room and made her way down the hall to the front foyer. A large circular stairwell rounded up the walls, highlighting a twenty-tiered crystal chandelier that dated to the creation of the house nearly a hundred years ago.

Tommy had just reached the top of the stairs. He didn't glance back as Nola silently climbed the stairs behind him. He stumbled down the hall and careened off one wall before bumping into another and then finally making it to his bedroom. He disappeared through the double doors.

Nola waited a few moments outside while Tommy stumbled to the bed and landed face down. She waited another few minutes, but there was no movement. He was well and truly out.

She smiled and then walked over to the closet in the hall. Pulling open the door, she looked down at the trunk that she had put together earlier in the day. Holes that she had carefully drilled lined the top. She lugged the trunk out and pulled it toward Tommy boy's bedroom. Once the trunk was clear of the doors, she shut them and got to work.

"OH, Tommy. Tommy boy. It's time to wake up." Nola slapped him hard across the face.

Tommy blinked, looking around. Then his eyes closed again.

Apparently he needed stronger measures. She reached into the shower, careful to stay to the side, and turned on the jets full blast.

The water was ice cold.

It only took another two seconds for Tommy's eyes to fly open wide with a yell.

Nola waited another few seconds before she turned off the stream, by which time Tommy was mumbling a series of curses. She grabbed a towel, drying off her arm.

"What the hell are you—" Tommy's words choked off, his eyes growing large as he stared straight ahead.

Nola gave him a moment to take in the scene. Snakes slithered along the floor of the glass container only a few feet away from him. There were only twelve of them, but Nola was sure that in Tommy's terrified mind, there were triple that.

There were three four-foot-long ball pythons in shades of brown, a half dozen king and milk snakes striped in red, white, and black that stretched to six or seven feet, and finally the three small orange corn snakes that topped out at only three feet. Nola had to admit that all mixed up together, it would be easy to mistake them for more than a mere dozen.

So completely focused on the snakes was he that Tommy hadn't even taken in his own position. Nola had strung him up to the nozzles in the shower. Helpfully, Tommy had a shower system with nozzles on both sides. His arms were stretched out above his head, his feet stretched at the same angle to the lower nozzles. It was a terrifying position to be in, even without the snakes.

Tommy pulled on his arms, and then his bloodshot eyes jolted, finally taking in his predicament.

His mouth went slack, his head turning to the side, making him look like a confused dog. He yanked on the ropes while trying to back away from the snakes. "Wh-what's going on?"

A wave of BO and beer breath wafted toward her. She grimaced at the smell. *Ugh. Apparently I should have dumped soap over him before I turned on the water.* She picked up the bat from where she'd leaned it against the wall. "Well, it seems you've been a rather bad boy, Tommy."

He yanked at his restraints, his gaze constantly darting back to the snakes. His words were slurred. "What? I didn't do nothing."

"Anything. You haven't done anything would be the correct way to say that. But either way, it's not true. You've done quite a bit. Do you remember Gina Torres?"

Fear flashed across his face before he attempted to cover it up. "I don't know her."

Nola shook her head. "Oh, you're not a good liar. How exactly have you managed to not get caught for something in all these years?"

Tommy attempted to puff up his chest, which was rather difficult given his current position. "I know the chief of police. You're going to be in so much trouble when I tell him—" A snake hissed, crawling along the side of the glass container.

Tommy's eyes widened, and he once again attempted to back up, which of course he couldn't do.

"Tell him what, Tommy? Are you going to describe me? Tell them I restrained you in your bathroom and then fed you to some snakes? You think they'll believe you?"

Tommy's voice shook. "Of-of course they'll believe me. So you better let me out right now."

"Not until we finish talking about Gina." Nola took a breath, trying to control her rage. "She was only eighteen. Did you know that? Did you know that before you raped her?"

Tommy glared, his eyes hard. "I didn't do anything she didn't want to do."

"Tell me, Tommy, do you know a lot of women who like to be hit? Who like to have their jaw broken while having sex?"

"She was into it."

Nola shook her head, not even sure why she was going down this road. Guys like Tommy thought that whatever they wanted, the woman wanted as well. Gina Torres had worked at the factory in New Brunswick. She was from Ecuador. She and her father had made the dangerous trip to America, but only Gina had made it all the way. Her father had been nabbed at the border and sent back. So Gina had been working for the last two years, sending as much money as she could back home. Of course, Tommy had swooped in every few weeks and taken half of her paycheck, which left precious little for her to send.

Nola pictured the crime scene photos of Gina. In life, she had been a beautiful young woman with dark hair and dark eyes. She'd also been incredibly small, not even reaching five feet. But that hadn't stopped Tommy, who was six foot three. Perhaps her small stature was what had drawn Tommy to her.

Gina had committed suicide a month ago. A friend of hers had written an anonymous blog post detailing the abuses that she'd experienced at Tommy's hand as well as Tommy's abuses of everyone in the factory. Bishop had found it and sent Nola along.

Nola gripped the bat clenched in her hand. Without another word, she walked over to the shower and swung. The bat connected with Tommy's ribs with a satisfying thud.

He screamed.

She swung again and again, aiming for the exact same spot. Tommy screamed and cried. After six swings, she stepped back.

Tommy sagged against the ropes, tears rolling down his cheeks. "Stop, just stop."

"Why should I, Tommy? From what I hear, you don't listen when other people tell you to stop, do you?"

"I told you, I haven't done anything."

Nola swung again, this time aiming at one of his knees. His high-pitched cry reverberated against the tiles.

Instead of eliciting sympathy, each sound angered Nola more. Men like this always acted tough, hiding behind their money. But when push came to shove, they were nothing.

She took a step back, needing to give herself some space from the weak man in front of her. "I have informants everywhere. I have a full accounting of what you've done at the factories. I have a full accounting of what you've done at the Gentleman's Club. And I know where you've hidden all your dirty money."

Tommy's head finally jolted up, his mouth fully open as his eyes widened. "What are you talking about?"

Nola would like to have been surprised that the one thing he cared about wasn't the crimes committed against people but the financial ones.

"I know you've been skimming off the top. You've been taking an extra ten grand a month out for the last three years. You take it from a different factory each time. That works out to close to a million dollars a year that you've been taking from your family's company. How do you think your dear old dad's going to view that?"

"He knows all about it."

Nola shook her head. "Oh, no, he doesn't. Or more accurately, no, he didn't. I sent him the files earlier today. He booked a flight for tomorrow morning. I also sent the files over to the feds."

"The feds? Why would they care?"

"You guys opened a factory in Pennsylvania last year. That means your crimes now extend across state borders, making it a federal matter. Know anybody at the federal level you can bribe?"

Tommy licked his lips. "We can work something out."

"No, we can't. It's already done. Now all that's left is the punishment."

Nola walked up to him, looking into his face. "Gina Torres killed herself because of you. You made her life hell. When you go to prison, I'll make sure that everyone inside knows what you did to her. They're not big fans of sex offenders in general pop."

Nola took a step back and then swung the bat in between his legs.

His face paled ten shades. He couldn't even manage a scream, just a small exhale of breath. She walked over to the other side of the bathroom and placed her hand on the glass container. "My sources say the feds will be by to get you in a few hours. Maria and Ava are already gone, so no one's coming for you until the feds arrive. But I don't want you to be lonely."

Tommy's eyes had been reduced to slits. The ropes were now all that were keeping him upright, but he managed to lift his head as Nola dragged the glass tank closer.

"It's funny how much you can learn about a person online. So many little reveals that they don't even know they're providing." Nola flicked the lid off the container.

The hissing grew louder now as the snakes slithered and moved across the bottom of the case. All the snakes were harmless, for the most part. The ball python, despite its name, wasn't large enough to ingest or squeeze Tommy. And generally, when scared or stressed, ball pythons looked for places to hide. Nola had looked at a few more dangerous ones, the kind that would wrap around a target and strangle them. It had been tempting, but she wanted a longer punishment for Tommy boy.

After all, she didn't want him dead. She just wanted him scarred.

"In the next few weeks, when you go to trial, remember that I will be watching. Remember that I will come back to visit you if you do anything but plead guilty to everything you have done."

Tommy dropped his head, sobs wracking his body. "No, no."

"Look at me," Nola demanded, taking a step toward him.

Tommy's eyes were now as big as saucers. He shifted his gaze from the snakes to Nola.

"If you even think about harming anyone else, I will come back. And you don't want me to come back, do you?"

Tommy shook his head.

Nola patted him on the cheek. "There's a good boy."

She turned and stepped out of the shower, stepping past the container. The image of Gina Torres in the bathtub of her small bathroom, blood staining the water, flashed through her mind. Nola kicked the side of the container.

It toppled over.

Snakes scrambled out, heading straight for the shower. Tommy began to scream in high-pitched wails. Nola didn't care. She turned and walked out of the bathroom, letting Tommy live in his nightmare. Gina Torres had had to live in her nightmare too. But she'd been so desperate to escape hers, she'd taken her own life.

Tommy couldn't escape his. Nola had made sure of that. He would only physically live in it for a few hours, but she knew the memory would stay with him forever.

It was the least he deserved.

CHAPTER TWO

RAFE

BREAKFAST DISHES WERE STILL on the table as Rafael Ortiz, aka Ralph Smith, walked into the kitchen. More dishes from last night were along the counter.

He ran his hands over his face. Both kids had woken up late. It had been a mad rush to get them out the door on time.

Last night, he'd let them stay up to watch the third *How to Train Your Dragon* movie that they'd picked up from the library. They all really liked that series of movies.

A quick glance at the clock told him he had about twenty minutes before he needed to head to the school himself. He was a janitor at Hempstead High School. He was only working a half day today because he worked overtime this weekend.

But he wanted to get in there early to see if he could start a little ahead of time and maybe get out earlier. If not, the kids would have to go to Mrs. Lee's house. He liked Mrs. Lee. She was a nice woman. And he appreciated her taking care of the kids when he got stuck working overtime, but he was really hoping he didn't have to pay for another babysitting stint. It was really beginning to dig into the small savings he'd managed to accumulate.

He needed to get home before the kids today. He needed to not spend money on a sitter if he was ever going to get them out of here.

Blowing out a breath, he looked around the apartment. The apartment was tiny, only about five hundred square feet. The front door opened directly into the living room, which at ten by twelve was the largest room in the place. Off the living room was a short hallway that led to the one bedroom and a small bathroom. Then there was a kitchen that boasted a small table and next to no counterspace. The walls, which had been painted white a few tenants ago, was now more of a dirty gray while the floor was a dirty brown. He didn't let the kids sit on the floor or even walk on it without shoes.

He didn't want much at this point, but a place where the kids could at least not wear their shoes indoors would be a nice change. But until he built up some more savings, that wasn't going to happen.

And he really needed the savings if he was ever going to get them out of this place.

They'd stayed in some of the worst places in Mexico when they'd been on the run from the cartel, but he wanted to be able to leave those days behind. He wanted the kids to be happy when they came home. He wanted the kids to each have their own room.

Although right now all three of them sleeping in the same bed was what they all wanted. No one wanted to let the others out of their sight.

He'd thought once he'd made contact with the US government, things would be better. And they were when compared to the nightmare of a trip from Mexico to the US. He knew he had it better than some immigrants, who walked for thousands of miles. But like many of them, they'd spent two months in line at the border. And that had been a short wait.

But the whole time, he'd been terrified that the cartel would find them. And there'd been no way to keep that terror from his kids. The day they'd been allowed across the border, a weight the size of a bus had lifted from his shoulders.

Getting the kids to go to school once they made it to America had been difficult though. He'd had to take the day off for the first two days in order to sit with Enzo so he felt comfortable. And then for the first month, he'd had to rush back to make sure he was there when school let out. Buses had been a whole new process for them to accept, but at least then it was the two of them together.

He sighed. He loved his kids. He wanted more than anything for them to be happy. But they still seemed to feel guilty whenever they laughed or smiled. As if somehow they were betraying the memory of their mother by letting some happiness into their lives.

Mariana wouldn't have wanted that. She would have wanted them to be happy. She would have *demanded* that they be happy.

Oh, Mariana, I miss you, he thought as he stared around the apartment. He'd found them a place to live, but it wasn't a home. Mariana had had a way of making any place they stayed feel like a home. Rafe wasn't sure if he had that skill in him. But he'd need to learn it. His kids needed a home, a place that they were happy to come back to. A place where they were comfortable.

At least he knew they were happy when they were with him. They felt safe when they were with him. He was grateful he'd been able to create that much for them. He hoped he could build on it so that they felt safer in this world in general.

As he walked over to the counter, he collected the plates from the table and placed them in the sink before putting the milk back in the refrigerator. The fridge only had leftover pizza and a carton of eggs. He closed the door. It looked like it would be scrambled eggs again for lunch. He'd leave the pizza for the kids tonight.

Rafe turned on the faucet, running a hand through the water, waiting for it to warm up.

A knock sounded at the front door.

He paused, glancing over his shoulder. People never knocked on doors in this neighborhood. As far as he could tell, that was a rarity in America in general.

He turned off the water, grabbing a towel from the bar on the stove. He walked to the living room as he dried off his hands.

But instead of going to the door, he went to the window next to it and pushed aside the curtain. Two police officers stood on his doorstep. He let the curtain fall back as a shiver ran through him.

This is America, not Mexico, he reminded himself.

Stuffing the towel in his pocket, he took a deep breath and unlocked the door. He pulled it open. "Can I help you?"

One of the officers was about Rafe's height of six foot three, but he had a few more years on him and a few extra pounds around the waist. He had pale skin and nearly white blond hair. His tag read Malcolm. His partner was younger. He couldn't be more than a few years older than twenty. He looked straight out of the academy. The younger officer glanced around, his eyes shifting, taking in everything.

Rafe estimated his age a little younger than he first thought. He was still jumpy from the get-go. He was the one that, if there were problems, he was where it would come from. The young ones always seemed to jump into problems before they were actually problems.

Officer Malcolm gave him a nod. "Mr. Smith?"

Rafe nodded. "Yes, I'm Ralph Smith."

Ralph Smith was the name he'd been given by the US authorities. He wasn't officially in the witness protection program yet, but the IDs were a first step. At the time, he thought the name Ralph was a bad choice. He'd never met a single Ralph in all the time he'd lived in Mexico. But he'd been so glad to get the IDs that he hadn't pushed the issue.

"Is it all right if we come inside for a moment? We have a few questions that we need to ask you," Malcolm said. His partner scanned the parking lot, his whole body tense.

Rafe looked beyond the officers to where their squad car had blocked his car in. Apparently they were making sure that he wasn't going anywhere. He knew time was ticking away, and the sooner he answered the police officers' questions, the sooner he could get to work. The dishes were going to have to wait. Mariana would not have been pleased.

He pulled the door open farther, stepping back. "Sure."

The officers stepped into the living room. The younger officer closed the door behind him.

"What's this about?" Rafe asked.

"There was an incident behind Hempstead High School two weeks ago. I'm sure you heard about it. We're talking to all of the staff to see if they saw anything."

Rafe had of course heard about the incident. A young boy, only fifteen, had been killed in the soccer field behind the school. Sadly, it was not an uncommon occurrence. Gang activity was rampant at Hempstead. MS-13 and the 18th Street gang had made their presence known.

Rafe turned toward the officers. "I'm afraid I can't—"

Malcolm pulled his weapon from his holster. "Hands up."

Rafe froze, staring at the man and then his partner, who also had his weapon cleared of his holster.

Slowly, Rafe raised his hands. "What's going on?"

"We're going to go for a little ride, Mr. Smith."

Rafe looked between the two of them. "Am I being charged with a crime?"

The younger officer smirked. "Yeah, sure. We can call it that."

Rafe shook his head. "I demand that a supervisor be called."

He knew his rights. He knew them backward and forward. He wasn't going anywhere with these two. Something was wrong about this. They hadn't even attempted to ask him a question. They hadn't even attempted to put handcuffs on him or read him his rights. None of this was procedure.

Malcolm waved the gun toward the door. "That's not going to happen. Get moving."

Rafe took a step back. What was with these guys? They should at least try to handcuff him.

He glanced at their belts and realized that both of them had placed their Tasers in the wrong spot. They were on the same side as their handguns. It was a sloppy mistake.

Plus, Malcolm was a little old for being a street cop. Not that it was impossible, but it just seemed unlikely. He should have been moved to a desk by now.

Rafe put up his hands. "Okay. I understand. But I left the water running in the kitchen. Let me just go turn it off."

Rafe took a step toward the kitchen. In the mirror above the couch, he saw the younger officer raise his weapon.

Rafe dove for the ground as a shot rang out. He slid along the floor and through the kitchen doorway, rolling to the side. More gunshots followed him. Heart pounding, he scrambled along the floor and behind the wall.

Sliding to his feet, his back against the wall, he grabbed the top of a chair from the kitchen table and pulled it silently toward him.

Malcolm stepped through the kitchen doorway. Rafe slammed the chair into the man's face. Then he grabbed Malcolm and bull-rushed him back through the doorway, using him as a shield.

His partner fired three shots. Two went into Malcolm's back. He screamed.

Rafe kept his hold on Malcolm and rushed him forward. He crashed him into the younger partner, pinning the man against the wall with Malcolm still in between them. The younger man's head slammed back into the door. He lost his grip on his gun.

Rafe slammed his fist into the kid's nose. It exploded in red.

Rafe let Malcolm drop but got tangled in his legs and had to back off. Recovered from his hit, the younger guy slid a switchblade from his back pocket. The knife sprang open with a click. He waved it in front of himself, demonstrating that he knew how to use it. Rafe pulled the kitchen towel from his pocket and wrapped one end around his hand. He waited until the kid made his move.

The kid struck, coming in with a sharp jab.

Rafe sidestepped the thrust, flicking the towel at the guy's face. The kid yelped as the towel made contact with his already broken nose.

Rafe grabbed the other side of the towel and in one fell swoop, wrapped it around the younger man's throat. He stepped behind him and pulled. The kid stumbled back.

Dropping down to one knee, Rafe kept pressure on the kid's throat as the kid's feet came up off the ground. With a final brutal tug, the kid's neck broke.

Rafe let the kid slide to the floor and then stumbled back. His breath came out in pants as he knelt looking at the two men on his floor. Blood stained the front of Malcolm's uniform. His partner's eyes stared out from his blood-covered face without blinking.

I killed them. Oh my God, I killed them.

He stumbled away from the bodies, his whole body shaking. His mind scrambled as he tried to figure out what had just happened and what he was going to do.

Calling the cops was out. They would take one look at the uniforms and not listen to a word that Rafe had to say.

He needed to call Juan Casteel, his contact in the US government. His eyes scanned the room for his cell phone. Where had he put it? Then he remembered he'd plugged it in to charge in the kitchen last night.

He stood up as movement from Malcolm caught the corner of his eye. Rafe's hope rose. *He's not dead, thank God.*

Malcolm grabbed the young man's gun.

Rafe took a step toward him. "No, don't—"

He pulled the trigger.

Rafe raced across the room, chased by bullets, but there was nowhere for him to go. The officers were blocking the door, and the kitchen had no exit.

Malcolm let off shot after shot. With no choice, Rafe dove out the living room window.

He hit the ground hard, rolling to ease some of the impact. He crashed into the fender of his Toyota. He got down on all fours, his whole body aching. He shook his head, looking up. A couple that had been crossing the parking lot stood staring at him, mouths agape.

Damn it. The choice of what to do now was out of his hands. He lumbered to his feet, feeling a twinge in his side. But he had no time for that. He didn't know what had just happened. He didn't know if those cops were legit or if the cartel had sent them.

Either way, they'd go for his kids next. He'd seen enough stories of how they treated brown kids in America to know that even if it was the government and not the cartel who got to them first, his kids would not be safe.

And if it was the cartel . . . He swallowed hard.

Holding his side, he hurried down the sidewalk. He needed to get to the kids. And then he needed to figure out what the hell they were going to do.

CHAPTER THREE

NOLA

THE CLOCK FACE showed one o'clock. Nola rolled over and stared at the unfamiliar ceiling of a Hampton Inn just off the New Jersey Turnpike. The walls were a pale ivory, the carpet a red-orange. She was surrounded by white pillows. She'd stacked them around her like a small fortress when she'd climbed into bed hours ago.

Shoving her dark-blonde hair from her face, she sat up, her mind still feeling a little groggy. She hadn't fallen asleep until close to seven. After leaving Tommy, she'd sent all of the information she had to Bishop with a note that the feds shouldn't hurry to his house. Then she'd gone to Denny's and gotten breakfast.

She stifled a yawn. This morning was the first sleep she'd had in nearly forty-eight hours. She'd planned on sleeping until late afternoon at least.

The light on her phone indicated what had woken her. Nola

rubbed her eyes as she squinted. Ileana Hamilton's name was displayed on the phone's screen.

"Huh," she mumbled. Ileana was her mother-in-law. From the moment Nola had met her, Ileana had treated her like she was a daughter, even before she started dating her son. They had worked together when Nola had been a CIA operative and Ileana had been in the top echelon of the intelligence hierarchy.

She had retired as the Director of National Intelligence a few years back, but she still remained a formidable woman.

Nola frowned. Ileana hadn't called her in . . . Actually, Nola couldn't remember the last time Ileana had called her. It was Bishop who made all the contacts. Of course, she'd seen Ileana when she had been brought to the estate after the situation in Georgia and the few times she'd been back in between, but still, this was unusual.

Trying to wipe away the remnants of sleep, Nola ran a hand over her face, then grabbed a hair tie from the side table. Pulling her hair into a messy bun, she stood up, stretched, reached for the phone, and dialed.

Ileana's voice came through the line crystal clear. "Morning, Nola," she said as if they regularly talked.

"Morning, Ileana. What's going on?" Nola walked over to the coffee maker, studying it. Did she dare risk making a cup? A news exposé she'd seen on what people did with the hotel coffee makers flashed through her mind. Nope, she'd get one downstairs.

"I have a bit of a favor to ask of you."

Nola sat back down on the bed. Ileana rarely asked for favors. She tended not to need them. But Nola knew better than to agree without hearing her out first. "I'm listening."

"I have a friend in the US Department of Justice. Rather high up."

Nothing about that was surprising. Ileana had friends everywhere.

"This friend has a case that could do a lot of good. But the agent in charge has gone missing. And their star witness . . . Well, two police officers were just found dead in his apartment."

Nola raised her eyebrows at that. "That's a bit of a problem."

"Yes," Ileana said dryly. "My friend doesn't believe that the witness is responsible for the death of the officers, or if he is, that he had good reason."

Nola was way too jaded to even try the argument that the cops must've been on the side of the right. There were plenty of good cops. Rascal Nealon from Georgia was a perfect example. But there were plenty who didn't deserve that moniker.

"I know you're nearby, and I was hoping you would be willing to go take a look. See if you could find the witness and secure him until my friend can find a safe way to bring him in."

"You want me to keep him from the police, I take it?"

"Until we know exactly what happened in that apartment, yes. I need you to keep him away from everybody. Just keep him hidden until we can figure out what the next steps are."

"Where is he?"

"Massapequa, New York."

Massapequa was on the southeastern shore of Long Island. It was about a two-hour car ride from where she was right now. But Long Island was a bit of a tricky beast. There were nine bridges on the western end that attached it to the mainland, as well as thirteen tunnels. They were almost always congested, painfully so at certain times of the day.

But they weren't the only way of getting on or off the island. Train lines and bus lines could as well. Out on the east side, the options for getting off the island were smaller, or at least the official ones. There were a few ferries that would take you over the

Long Island Sound. And of course, if you could access a boat, you could leave the island that way.

"When did this happen?" Nola asked.

"About five to six hours ago."

Nola shook her head. "If your guy's any good, he'll already be off the island."

"If he were on his own, yes. But he has his two children with him. They're young and will slow him down. Plus, my contact doesn't think he'll be willing to risk their safety. It'll make him cautious."

Nola stood up again, glancing around the room, taking stock of what she'd need to pack and how quickly she could be out the door. "Okay, I'll be on the road in about fifteen minutes."

"Excellent. I'll have Bishop contact you with the dossier."

Nola headed toward the bathroom. "You never told me. What's this guy's name?"

"Rafael. Rafael Ortiz."

NOLA WAS REALLY MISSING the plane right now. On paper, the trip from New Jersey to Massapequa was only about seventy miles, all highway. It should have taken a little over an hour at most.

But that, of course, didn't account for the disaster that was traffic in Queens.

Nola drummed her hands on the steering wheel. She was caught on the Cross Bronx Expressway, which had to be the world's worst road. It seemed like everybody in Queens was trying to get on it at the same time.

Traffic moved forward inch by painful inch. At this rate, it would take three days to get out to the eastern end of Long Island.

Her phone rang, and she quickly answered. "Hey, Bishop."

"Hey, Nola, how you doing?"

She and Bishop had come a long way in the last few months. After the case down in Georgia, Nola had spent a week at the estate. It had been both good and completely horrible to be back home.

But seeing Bishop again, that had been good. She had been wrong to cut Bishop out of her life. Bishop was hurting over the death of Molly and David as much as Nola was. They had been Bishop's first true family, and then Nola had walked away from her as well. The pain of that must've been excruciating.

Nola was trying to make up for it now. She wasn't ready to come back and have things be like they were. But a phone call every now and then wasn't too much to ask.

Nola slammed on her brakes as a BMW scooted into her lane with no warning and only a few inches to spare. She swallowed down the angry tirade that wanted to burst from her lips. But she couldn't resist giving the arrogant ass a one-finger salute. "I'm good. What's the situation with the Cameron family?"

"Tommy was taken into federal custody three hours ago. And one of the prosecutors got wind of his activities at the factories involving the immigrants. The attorney's going to keep immigrants' identities and statuses secret but will file charges that range from harassment to theft to rape."

Nola closed her eyes for a moment, breathing deep. "Gina wasn't the only girl."

The pain in Bishop's voice was as obvious as the anger. "As we both know, those kinds of predators are never happy with just one victim."

Nola sighed, shifting in her seat. She wished that she didn't know that. She wished that her life was untouched by all the pain and horror that she knew and understood all too well. But she had learned at an early age that people could be cruel. Not because they had to be, but because they wanted to be.

And while she'd had a short break away from that cruelty for a few years with David and Molly, that break had been an illusion. And she had dragged the two people she loved the most into her nightmare. The cold, dark feeling that fell over her at those thoughts was sadly comforting. This cold, dark place was where she lived. It was where she'd lived for the last two and a half years. And as far as Nola could tell, it would be where she lived until she finally joined Molly and David.

"So I've got some more information on your target."

"Okay. What do you know?"

"His name is Rafael Ortiz. Although he goes by Ralph Smith in the United States."

"Where'd he get that name?"

"Government provided," Bishop said. "He's in the process of being put into the witness protection program. He'd been granted immediate emergency asylum along with his two kids, Sofia, age eight, and Enzo, age six."

Her breath caught at the mention of Rafael's little girl. A vision of Molly with bright-red ribbons in her dark hair flashed through her mind. She flipped a glance in the rearview mirror. Molly looked up at her and smiled and then went back to playing with her doll.

Nola cleared her throat. "Why was he given asylum?"

"He's a former police detective from Tijuana. He offered to testify against the cartel."

Nola let out a low whistle. Tijuana was the frontline of the fight against drug cartels. No matter what side you were on with the cartels, for or against them, life was violent and brutal. Tijuana had the dubious distinction of being one of the most dangerous cities in the world. On average, there were over 2,000 homicides annually. Thanks in part to the intervention of the

Mexican army and the national guard, the trend had been ticking downward, but Tijuana still held the distinction of having the most homicides in all of Mexico.

"So who is he really?" Nola asked.

"A unicorn, actually. He was a good cop in the middle of a drug war. He offered to turn state's evidence against one of the cartel's leaders after they killed a DEA agent. He'd slowly been gathering evidence against the cartels for years. The cartel found out. His wife was killed before they could escape. He managed to make it out with his two kids and get across the border."

"Brave. Doesn't sound like the kind who would kill a cop for no good reason."

"Unless, of course, he's suffering from some sort of PTSD."

Nola knew that was possible. Trauma and violence often had long-term effects, PTSD now becoming one of the better known. And with PTSD and any serious brush with violence, paranoia was not unusual.

"There didn't seem to be any indication of PTSD. But the referral psych eval hadn't been completed yet," Bishop said.

"What do we know about the cops?"

"One of them had their neck broken. The other one was shot in the back multiple times."

Nola winced, trying and failing to come up with a good explanation for that.

Bishop continued. "Apparently one of the officers managed to get a few shots off before Ortiz dove through the living room window."

Well, that was violent. "Any sightings of him since?"

"Only one. He was last seen at his kids' school. He went straight from his apartment to the school and took them out. And then he disappeared."

"His car?"

"Still at the apartment. The police officers boxed it in before they went after him."

"What about his handler?"

"Juan Casteel. Still can't find him. People are beginning to get a little worried."

Nola frowned. It seemed like an awfully big coincidence that Casteel went missing just as Ortiz lost his mind. "Why did the cops stop by his apartment?"

"There was a murder behind the high school where Rafe works. The officers were going over there to ask him some questions."

"Was he a suspect?"

"I don't know. Hempstead PD has closed ranks. They're not really revealing anything."

"Hempstead. That's got a heavy gang problem. Isn't MS-13 pretty busy in that area?"

"Yeah," Bishop said. "They've been active there for a while. In fact, there was another killing at the school only a few months back. Two members of the 18th Street gang, an MS-13 rival, were charged."

Nola knew the 18th Street gang had started in Los Angeles and was composed of mainly Mexicans and Central Americans. Not as well-known as MS-13, the 18th Street gang was just as violent and were also fond of their head-to-toe tattoos. The 18th Street gang's recruiting techniques often targeted middle school and even elementary school students. A large number of members ended up in US prisons, which only became a recruitment breeding ground for them. Deportations similarly had an unintended consequence of spreading their reach throughout Central America.

Traffic continued to inch forward. A spot opened up to Nola's left. She quickly changed lanes. Now she was cruising at a speedy ten miles per hour, but it felt like she was flying compared to before.

Ahead, she saw the exit for the Throgs Neck Bridge, and she said a quiet prayer of thanks. She quickly made her way over to the exit. "Okay, finally getting off the road from hell. If the bridge isn't too bad, I should hopefully be there in about forty-five minutes."

"He's been on the run for almost six hours."

"Any activity on his cell phone or accounts?"

"Before going to the kids' school, he went to the bank and withdrew all of his money. His cell phone was still at the apartment."

If he was a police detective, he might have a better idea of how to hide than the average person. But people always left clues.

"Crime scene?"

"It hasn't been released yet. But I've got pictures online. I'll send them to you."

Nola nodded as she turned on to the exit. *Okay, Detective Ortiz, let's see where you're hiding.*

CHAPTER FOUR

NOLA

THE APARTMENT COMPLEX of Rafael Ortiz was right on the edge of the Massapequa border. It had been built back in the 1980s and looked like it hadn't been updated since. There were forty apartments spread across three separate buildings on two stories. Most of the apartments were one-bedroom spreads with a few two-bedrooms. The apartment complex catered to people on the lower-income spectrum.

According to what Bishop had sent her, not a lot of crime had been reported in the area, at least not a lot that was perpetrated by the people living in the apartment complex. But there seemed to have been their fair share of victimization here.

It was a good forty-minute drive to his job over in Hempstead. But Massapequa had one of the better school districts in Long Island. She wondered if that was why Ortiz had chosen it.

Nola sat in the parking lot, her lights off, as she studied the complex. People hurried by watching their surroundings, not paying too much attention to what other people were doing unless those people came near them.

When she'd driven into the parking lot, she doubted any of the neighbors had gotten to know Ortiz and his family. A canvass of those neighbors had revealed that to be true. The Ortizes, or Smiths as they were known here, had only been here a few months.

But Nola had managed to speak with one neighbor who had gotten to know the family. Mrs. Lee was a seventy-two-year-old Korean woman who lived two doors down from the Ortizes. She'd been beside herself when she'd heard about the deaths in Ortiz's apartment and kept repeating that it wasn't possible that he had done that. That he was a good man.

As far as Nola was concerned, the jury was still out on that. Besides, she knew even good men could do horrible things.

Nola had gone back to her car after the interview with Mrs. Lee. Then she waited for it to get a little bit darker. Now it was 4:30, and the sun had slunk below the horizon. The light bulb she'd taken out from the hallway in front of Ortiz's home had left his front door in darkness. There was yellow crime scene tape over the door but no officer stationed. Massapequa didn't have a big police department, and the scene had already been processed. Besides, as far as they could tell, they knew exactly who the offender was.

Nola slipped out of the car, no light giving away her position. She'd already turned off the interior light.

She quietly made her way across the parking lot and down the long sidewalk. The apartment complex had actually been a hotel complex back in the 1980s that catered to people interested in going to the beach, so all the apartments had doors that led directly into the parking lot. From what she'd seen in Mrs. Lee's apartment, it looked as if the company that had converted it had simply combined two small motel rooms together to create the units. The second bathroom had been converted into a kitchen. It was not a place that would be easily called home. There was a transitional quality to it, as if people simply lived there long enough to get enough money so that they didn't have to live there anymore.

As Nola stepped to the Ortizes' door, she slipped her lock-pick from her back pocket. A quick glance around showed that no one was in the area. She yanked off the police tape and made quick work of the lock, only needing to feel the tumblers. Ten seconds later, she was inside and closing the door behind her.

She pulled out her flashlight and scanned the room. A fight had definitely occurred here. The furniture, what little there was of it, was pushed around. There was a large bloodstain only three feet from the door. Bullet holes dotted the wall opposite the front door leading into the kitchen.

Nola frowned at the holes. Obviously Rafe had attempted to get away from the officers, and they had opened fire.

But why open fire? Police officers couldn't just shoot because a perp wasn't listening to them.

Maybe he had a weapon? She couldn't rule it out. A knife was a definite possibility, if he hadn't managed to snag himself a black-market gun.

She walked into the kitchen, flashing her light around the kitchen, which for the most part was undisturbed, except for one chair that was missing from the kitchen table. From what she'd read of the report, they'd bagged the chair. Apparently Ortiz had struck one of the officers with it.

But why do that if he had a weapon?

It would make more sense for him to shoot back. And the officers must've been following him into the kitchen. They couldn't have been taken unaware. Unless he'd made them back off after he'd taken a shot at one of them? But there were no bullet holes by the front door. And where the heck did the broken chair come into the mix?

Nola shook her head. Something wasn't adding up.

The kitchen still had breakfast dishes in the sink. Flies now circled above them. She ran her flashlight over the kitchen counter, but for the most part it was pretty neat besides the dirty dishes. Her hands gloved, she opened the refrigerator. Pizza, eggs, and one carton of milk. She opened up the freezer. Nothing but ice cube trays. Closing the door, she stood looking around the kitchen. It was like they had just moved in yesterday.

Or they simply didn't have a lot of extra money to be spending on food or decorations.

Once again, that didn't make sense. The federal government, if he was a witness, should have been providing him with enough funds.

But being he wasn't officially in the witness protection program, he wouldn't be getting his utilities paid for. He was supporting two kids on a janitor's salary in one of the worst school districts on Long Island. So he definitely wasn't making much money from Hempstead. But he'd chosen to live in Massapequa, which meant his kids went to one of the better schools on Long Island.

She made her way down the hall. A quick glance in the bathroom showed what you would you expect: toothbrushes, toothpaste, shampoo, conditioner, and two towels.

The bedroom indicated that the children slept in there with him. One large bed with a Mickey Mouse comforter on it. There were two stuffed animals on the bed carefully tucked under the blankets, their heads on the pillow. Obviously one of the kids had tucked them safely in before leaving for school that morning.

The room didn't have much by way of decorations except for a few hand-drawn pictures. Nola stepped closer to one that caught her attention. It was of a man with a little girl and a little boy. And floating up above them was an angel with long yellow hair.

A family portrait.

She scanned the room, but there wasn't much to go on. She flipped open the dresser and saw only a handful of shirts and pants between the two kids.

Mr. Ortiz was definitely struggling to make ends meet.

Had the abysmal accommodations finally gotten to him? Had he decided that he needed to find a more lucrative job? Had that brought trouble to his door?

She shook her head and stepped back into the hall, doing one more search of the apartment, but she found nothing new.

A glance at her watch showed that it was getting close to five o'clock. The high school should be emptied out by now. On impulse, she walked back to the bedroom and grabbed the two stuffed animals before leaving the apartment.

Tucking the bear and puppy into her jacket, she quickly made her way across the parking lot and into her truck. She shivered as she started up the engine. It felt like with the sun gone, the temperature had plummeted another ten degrees.

Two men were headed out of the far side of the lot now. They glanced up but then looked away, not seeming concerned about her.

She placed the two stuffed animals in the backseat. She'd grabbed them on impulse just in case she found Rafe and his kids. The kids were in for a rough couple of days. They might need some friends.

CHAPTER FIVE

NOLA

HEMPSTEAD HIGH SCHOOL had the unfortunate distinction of being one of the worst on Long Island. Its graduation rate had only recently risen above thirty-seven percent, among the lowest in the nation. Corruption was rife, and there was even a convicted pedophile allowed to roam the halls. In fact, there were a number of corrupt individuals linked to the school, including a disgraced former cop who was still able to sit on the school board. To make matters more difficult, seventy percent of Hempstead students were on some sort of public assistance, and only sixty percent were proficient in English.

And then, of course, there were the gangs.

Nola's phone rang just as she placed her hand on the door handle of her car. She answered it after a quick glance at the screen. "Hey, Bishop. What have you got for me?"

"Something . . . odd."

Nola settled back in her seat. "Okay. Tell me."

"Well, I got a little further in figuring out why the police were going to speak with Ortiz. It seems he was a suspect in the murder of the fifteen-year-old behind the soccer field."

Nola frowned. "I thought that was gang related?"

"It is. The victim was the brother of a known MS-13 gang member. The cops think the killing was in response to MS-13 killing a lieutenant in the 18th Street gang."

Nola was familiar with the rivalry. Both gangs were brutal and violent. In the 1990s, when members of both gangs started to get deported in increasing numbers, they became rival criminal factions in their home countries of El Salvador, Honduras, and Guatemala. Both had members spanning from Central America up through Canada. And both engaged in kidnapping, drug trafficking, prostitution, money laundering, and contract killings. The rivalry between the two came to high point in 2014, when fourteen people were being killed daily in El Salvador.

"So how does it tie to Ortiz?"

"The working theory is that Ortiz was trying to get into MS-13 and that he killed fifteen-year-old Danny as an initiation."

Nola frowned as she stared out at the parking lot, watching a group of kids toss a basketball between them as they headed for a car. "Ortiz is thirty-seven years old, right?"

"Yep."

"And he's from Mexico, right?"

"Yup."

"Does he have any ties to Ecuador or Guatemala?"

"Nope."

"And he's a former police detective?"

"Yup."

"That's the stupidest theory any police officer has ever come up with. He's too old. He's from the wrong country, and he's a former cop. A cop who lost his wife to gang activity. Why on earth would they think he was actually interested in joining the gang?"

"No idea. But that's what the word is now."

Nola rubbed her forehead, trying to figure out what the heck was going on. There was no way a thirty-seven-year-old former police detective decided now was the time to join a gang, especially when he was responsible for his two kids and his wife had been killed by gang members.

So then why would—

She went still, a single possibility coming to mind. "Bishop, where did the cops get the info about Ortiz being a member of a gang?"

"Anonymous source."

Nola groaned. *Oh crap.* Already the news was full of stories about a cop killer on the loose flashing Ortiz's face. "Which means MS-13 is going to be out looking for Ortiz along with the cops. He can't run to the bad guys, and he can't run to the good guys. He's stuck in the middle."

"No legitimate source will help him, and all the illegitimate sources will be too scared of MS-13 to even think of crossing them," Bishop said.

"Yup."

It was a nice little box that Rafael and his family had now been placed in. He was officially in a damned if he did, damned if he didn't position.

But the thing was, Ortiz would have known that this would happen. He wasn't a stupid guy. If he did kill those cops, he had to have known what the fallout would be. So why did he do it?

"Okay. Let me know if you learn anything else."

"Will do. And, Nola, I know I don't have to say it, but the cops are going to be trigger-happy, and MS-13 is always machete happy, so be careful, okay?"

"I will." She disconnected the call. She pictured Rafael and his family. He'd stepped on a landmine back in his apartment, and the shrapnel was still flying. The repercussions of this were huge. She was amazed he'd managed to stay hidden for this long. But if she didn't find him soon, someone else was going to find him, that was for sure. Too many people were out looking for him now.

She stepped out of the car, slamming the door behind her. *Rafael, whatever hole you've hidden yourself in, I hope it's deep.*

CHAPTER SIX

RAFE

RAFE USHERED Sofia and Enzo into the motel room. He stopped at the door, glancing outside, but no one was paying him any attention. At this hotel, he had the feeling people tried not to pay attention to others. The rooms were rented by the hour, and where people stayed wasn't a priority.

And I brought my kids here. He closed the door and then leaned against it.

Sofia, her eyes looking even darker today, looked up at him. "What's wrong, Papa?"

Rafe forced a smile to his face. "Nothing, my love."

"Why are we here? Aren't we going back to the apartment?"

She always said "the apartment," never home. And she was right, the apartment wasn't home. Home was back in Mexico with her mother.

Rafe hated that they were in this rat nest of a hotel, but he simply didn't know where else to take them. When he'd taken them out of school, he'd struggled with where to go. It seemed like there were cameras everywhere these days. The train stations were out, as were any other forms of public transport. From their school, he'd taken them for a long walk. When they'd gotten tired, he'd had to risk a bus ride.

Even then, he wasn't sure where to take them. But he needed to go somewhere they hadn't been before. They ended up on a bus to Riverhead and had wandered around the outlet mall there for a few hours. He'd bought them hats to try and help keep their faces from the cameras. He wasn't worried so much about their faces as his own.

But he'd tucked Sofia's hair up in her hat to make it appear at a quick glance that she was a boy. Up close, she wouldn't fool anyone. Those giant deep eyes of hers would give her away.

Now those eyes stared at him, wanting to know what was going on.

Sofia was eight, but she was much older than her years. She had been forced to grow up fast. First because of his job as a policeman in Mexico City. Mariana, his wife, had been full of life and energy, but she was never very good at hiding her emotions. Sofia had taken on the role of assuring her that everything would be all right.

And once Mariana had died, Sofia had taken on the role of mother to Enzo. Rafe hated that he was forcing her to grow up so fast.

But he supposed that was better than what he had done to poor Enzo. Enzo had barely said more than a dozen words a day since his mother had been killed. He was locked away somewhere inside himself. He drew away from people, not trusting them.

Rafe didn't know of any other way to help break Enzo out of the state that he was in. But they had been making strides. His teacher had told him that Enzo had finally made some friends. He had two kids, a boy and a girl, he now sat with regularly at lunch. It was such a small thing, and yet for Rafe that was the greatest thing he had heard since he'd come to this country—that his son had friends.

And now I've ruined that too.

He forced a smile to his face. "Are you guys hungry?"

They shook their heads in unison. They were rarely hungry these days. All they'd had were small meals or no meals since they'd left Mexico. He was pretty sure their stomachs had shrunk so they now required less food than they did only a few months earlier.

Oh God, Mariana, how did I screw this up so badly?

But he knew the answer to that. He couldn't take the bribes. When he was a police officer, it was commonplace in his department for officers to look the other way when the gangs and cartels struck.

But Rafe had been unable to do that. He'd seen kids slaughtered, and there was no accountability. There was no remorse. And then the next week it would just be another slaughter. People lived in fear of the cartels harming them and those they loved, so much that they went along, creating fear in others.

He couldn't be part of that cycle. He'd needed to do something. He needed to try and make the world a slightly better place for his children.

So he'd started taking notes. He'd started gathering evidence. He thought he was being so slick, so careful. But somewhere along the way, someone realized what he was doing.

Bullets had rung through his kitchen window one night just as they'd all sat down for dinner. He'd yanked Sofia and Enzo to the ground, covering them with his body.

But Mariana . . . God, Mariana. He could still see her face staring at him, her beautiful eyes open but seeing nothing.

And if he was still living with that image, he had no doubt his children were as well. They'd been on the run for two months after that before he managed to reach out to someone in the US Department of Justice. They'd brought them over the border and tucked them in a hotel in Phoenix for six months.

He'd been interviewed over and over, going over all of the details. But he'd refused to hand over the evidence he had until he had a deal in writing. He slipped his hand into his pocket, feeling the flash drive there. He kept it on him at all times.

And thank God for that. If he'd left the apartment without it, he would be completely sunk. Now he knew the flash drive was the only chance his family had.

After Phoenix, they'd been moved to Long Island, still not officially in the witness protection program. There were a few more obstacles that he needed to overcome, like testifying. As soon as they had a court date, his status would be official.

That had been four months ago. Now he felt like he'd been hung out to dry. He knew that wasn't the case. He knew that cartel cases were serious, complex, and dangerous. Not just to the witnesses but to everyone from the prosecutors to the defense attorneys to the judge, and just about everybody involved in any way, shape, or form.

And now that danger had come home to him. It had come home once again to his family.

He pushed himself away from the door. "You want to watch some TV?"

Sofia looked into his eyes and then nodded, taking her brother's hand. "Come on, Enzo. We'll find something good to watch."

Once again, the little mother had emerged. Sofia got Enzo settled on the bed, and then she hopped up next to him, grabbing the remote and flicking through channels like a pro.

Rafe watched them for a few minutes after bolting the door and putting a chair in front of it. He walked to the bathroom and glanced inside. It was beyond basic and probably not very clean, but he needed a minute alone. "I'll be right in here, okay, guys?"

"Okay, Papa," Sofia said, her eyes still glued to the screen.

He closed the door, and after closing the lid, sat down on the toilet. He lowered his head into his hands.

I killed two cops.

His hands started to shake. They'd come to his apartment, but everything about it had been wrong. At the same time, he couldn't help but think that maybe *he* had been wrong. Had he been so paranoid from his time in Mexico that he just assumed all cops were corrupt now?

He'd gotten a bad feeling from them, but he'd had a bad feeling about every cop he'd worked with in Mexico by the time he'd left.

In his mind, he went over the scenario again. The officers at the door. Them coming in, drawing their weapons without asking a question. Everything about them still seemed wrong. But he could no longer tell if that was because it was wrong or because he'd just convinced himself that it was.

He supposed on many levels it didn't matter. If they were bad cops, if they were good cops, the result for him was the same: He was a cop killer. One from Mexico. No one was going to see beyond that.

He pulled out the burner phone he'd picked up. Should he call Casteel? He just didn't know. Would Casteel even believe him?

Oh God, what do I do?

CHAPTER SEVEN

NOLA

HEMPSTEAD HIGH SCHOOL was not a model institute for the achievement of today's youth. But as Nola stepped inside, it was hard to tell the difference between this high school and thousands of others across the United States.

She stopped in at the front office, but no one was around, so she wandered the halls looking for Harry Schiller, the other janitor. She knew where the janitors' closets were, but they were literally just closets, not offices, so she knew she wouldn't find Harry there. She finally came across him in the large gym. He was mopping the floor.

Nola crossed the wooden floor. Her footsteps echoed through the open space, but Harry didn't look up. According to public records, he was fifty-eight years old and had worked for the district for twenty-five years. With red hair slowly turning to white, he was definitely on the pale side and very slim. He looked up when Nola approached, his eyes bloodshot. It looked like good old Harry might have a drinking problem.

Harry shoved his mop into the bucket. "Can I help you with something?"

The question was gruff and not exactly welcoming.

"I'd like to talk to you about Ralph Smith."

Harry grunted, pulling the mop back out and continuing to clean the floor. "You a cop? Because they've already been by here."

"I'm not a cop."

Harry looked up, a shrewd look coming across his face. "A reporter?"

Nola slipped the fifty from her back pocket and handed it over. "Does it really matter who I am?"

Harry took the fifty and then slipped it into his pocket with a shrug. "I suppose it doesn't. What do you want to know?"

"What did you think about Ralph?"

Harry shrugged again. "He's Mexican," he said, as if that explained everything.

"I'm going to need a little bit more than that."

After rinsing out the mop head, Harry leaned on the end of the mop handle. "He came here what, four months ago? He works all right, I suppose, but you know those Mexicans. They're always looking for a handout. Probably came here illegally. Not that the school district cares. You know, people like me, we've been working here for decades, and then these immigrants come in and start taking our jobs. It's not right."

Nola ignored all the prejudice. It wasn't an accurate summation of Rafael Ortiz's personality, merely exposition on Harry Schiller's worldview. "Did you ever see anything specific that made you think he couldn't be trusted?"

"Like I said, none of them can be trusted."

Nola stared at him.

He shrugged, his gaze shifting to his bucket. "No, I suppose he didn't really do anything specific that made him untrustworthy. He was sneaky like that. Whatever he was doing, it wasn't in plain sight."

Nola decided to switch tack. "I hear that Hempstead has a gang problem."

Harry snorted. "A gang *problem*? That's like saying a leopard has a spot problem."

"Any reason to think that Rafe was mixed up in that?"

Harry shrugged again. "Well, he's Mexican so . . ."

Right. Helpful. "Does Ralph have a locker?"

Harry nodded. "Yeah."

"I'd like to see that."

He peered at Nola. "It's going to cost you extra to see that."

Nola didn't even bother rolling her eyes. She'd gotten Harry's take the minute he'd first looked up. The world had treated him unfairly. And it was all the fault of someone else. Right now, that someone else seemed to be immigrants.

Of course, the four DUIs that he'd gotten, which caused him to lose his license, wasn't their fault. Neither was the divorce that happened ten years ago or the fact that he was so far behind in his child support payments that the court had cut off his visits with his children the decade before. His son had just graduated college, and his daughter had just started. He'd missed all of that.

But it was immigrants that were really causing all of Harry's problems.

Nola pulled out another twenty bucks and handed it over. Harry looked at it and then at her. This time she was the one who shrugged. "It's all I've got."

He stared at it a moment before shoving it in his pocket. "Fine. It's time for my break anyway."

Harry led the way across the floor. "You know, Ralph was

supposed to be doing this. But he didn't show up this morning. Typical," he said gruffly.

Nola knew that wasn't actually true. Ralph had been given the morning off because he had worked on Saturday. Hempstead didn't have a lot of funds, so rather than paying overtime, they paid in time off.

Luckily, that was the end of Harry's attempts to make conversation. He led the way down the hall and around the corner. There was a door marked "stairs," and he opened it. Everything inside was dark. Harry reached in and tugged on a chain attached to a single light bulb. The small light illuminated dark concrete walls and an old wooden set of stairs.

Harry hustled down the stairs, holding on to the railing. Nola followed. A small area had been carved out into a makeshift workroom. Tools and equipment lined three rows of shelves. A long worktable was to the side of them and lockers on the other side. Boilers took up the other side of the room.

Harry waved toward the locker on the far left. "Had a lock on it. Cops snipped it earlier. Not sure if there's anything left. I need to get back to work. Don't look at anything else," he said with a glare before heading back up the stairs.

Nola watched him go, waiting until he'd reached the top step before she opened the locker. She knew she was unlikely to find anything of interest, being the cops had already been here.

Inside the locker, a single uniform shirt hung. An old water bottle lay at the bottom of the locker. And there was nothing else. The cops had cleared it all out. Damn it.

She reached up along the top shelf of the locker but didn't feel anything. She pulled out the shirt, turning it this way and that, but it gave her nothing either.

Pulling out her flashlight, she inspected the bottom of the locker. There was something along the right-hand corner. It looked like a piece of paper caught in the side of the locker. Only about an inch of it was visible. She had a feeling that in the cops' haste to search the locker, they'd dislodged it, and it slipped down. She carefully fished it out.

It was a picture of Rafe Ortiz and his family. He was a tall muscular man with dark hair and dark eyes. He stood smiling at the camera with his arm around a beautiful blonde woman with blue eyes and tan skin. Standing in front of them were two small children. All four of them beamed at the camera. It was a beautiful shot. It was a family caught in a happy moment.

"They look happy."

Nola turned around to find Molly sitting on top of the workbench, her feet kicking away.

"Yeah, they do."

"The mom's gone now. The kids are sad."

"How do you know the kids are sad?"

"Why wouldn't they be? They love their mommy."

Nola looked down at the picture and then slipped it into her pocket.

"Do you think the daddy's a bad man, Mommy?"

"I don't know, baby."

"The kids aren't bad, are they?"

"No, baby. They're not bad."

"You're going to help them, aren't you?"

"I'm going to try."

CHAPTER EIGHT

BISHOP

BISHOP SAT in her little cubbyhole at Langley. As part of the Directorate of Science and Technology, Bishop Rhodes was a large part of the collection, synthesis, and analysis of information that was on the frontline of coordinating US actions with allies overseas.

It sounded impressive. And the work she did was important, but her workspace definitely did not indicate it. She sat in a five-by-five gray cubby, complete with a cat poster encouraging her to hang in there. The poster was a remnant from the previous cubby resident, but she'd grown fond of it.

On her desk sat three monitors, a keyboard, mouse, and cupholder. Bishop rarely worked with paper. Everything she worked on involved electronic files and investigations.

But the US government had been underutilizing her skill. She was young, so she thought that was probably part of the reason that they didn't realize all she could do. But the bright side of that was it left her time to back up Nola.

Ever since Georgia, things with Nola had been changing. It wasn't perfect. It wasn't like she'd decided to come home for good, but they were definitely getting better. They talked almost every week now. Granted, it was pretty much just Bishop giving her details and Nola taking them in, but it was a lot more communication than she'd had for the last two years. And Bishop would take whatever she could get.

"Bishop, we're going to get something to eat. You coming?" Stan Mahoney looked over the divider and down at Bishop with a hopeful expression on his face. Stan was thirty years old and prematurely balding with glasses. He was also an absolute whiz on the computer. And he was a genuinely nice guy. Bishop normally had lunch with him and two other analysts.

But not today.

She shook her head. "Can't. I'm in the middle of something."

"Want me to bring you back something?"

"Yeah. Maybe a meatball sub?" She reached into her bag hanging on the back of her chair to pull out some money.

Stan waved her away. "I got it. You get me the next time I get caught up."

Bishop smiled her thanks, and Stan disappeared from over her divider.

She turned her attention back to the life of Ralph Smith, aka Rafael Ortiz.

So far she liked the guy. He had been a decorated officer in Tijuana, which was probably what landed him with a target on his back. He'd been in hiding with his family for close to a year now. She hadn't been able to get anything from the handler's files.

But she had been able to grab some pictures from social media, though. His wife's accounts hadn't been shut down after her death. They showed a pretty, happy family. The kids were awfully cute.

Ortiz's work history showed no excessive force, no questionable decisions. Killing those two cops seemed really out of character.

She glanced at her phone, wondering if it was worth it to put in another call to Juan Casteel, Ortiz's handler. She'd been trying to reach him for the last couple of hours. In fact, a lot of people had been trying to reach him for the last couple of hours. Nobody seemed to have had any luck. It was like Juan Casteel had disappeared from the face of the earth.

And Bishop didn't think that was a coincidence.

The question was whether he was involved in whatever Ortiz was up to or whether he was a victim of it.

Bishop ran some more searches as she sat back, sipping on her coffee. *What happened to you, Casteel? What are you—*

A beep sounded on her monitor. She quickly righted herself, spilling some of her coffee. "Crap." She shoved her seat back, avoiding the coffee splash. Shaking her head at her clumsiness, she placed the mug on the desk and searched the screen to see what had popped up.

And it looked like Juan Casteel had popped up.

His body had been found off the Brooklyn-Queens Expressway near Union Street and Hamilton Avenue. From the description, though, it was clear that was where he had been dumped, not where he had been killed. He'd been shot point blank in the head, but his body showed evidence of torture. There were welts along his chest and burn marks on his feet.

Damn, Casteel, who got to you?

It was possible it was unrelated to Ortiz's case. Casteel had been working a few different cases, all of them high level, all of them violent. But the timing was just too much to overlook.

Another beep sounded on Bishop's other monitor. She

glanced at it with a frown. She turned her chair, quickly typing on her keyboard, and pulled the information up.

Someone had just called Casteel's work phone. Bishop had been monitoring his phones for the past couple of hours. So far everything had been pretty standard.

But this call was from a motel out on the eastern end of Long Island, about forty minutes from where Ortiz had killed those two cops.

Bishop grabbed the phone and dialed quickly.

CHAPTER NINE

NOLA

NOLA DID another search of Rafe's locker but didn't find anything else. She stood back staring at the empty locker and then glanced over at Harry's. *Don't look at anything else.*

Slipping her lockpick kit out of her back pocket as she moved in front of Harry's locker, she quickly got it open. Grabbing a screwdriver from the workbench, she poked through the top shelf, which held at least two very pungent shirts. A clank sounded from the back-right corner.

Wrinkling her nose, she shifted the shirts aside. Tucked in the back corner was a bottle of Jack. Shocking.

She also found a jacket that looked way too big for Harry but looked like it would just about fit Ortiz. Apparently Harry had cleaned out Rafe's locker before the cops arrived.

There was also a book, *The Power of One* by Bryce Courtenay. Nola had read it years ago. It was about a young bullied

English boy growing up in South Africa, a tale about overcoming adversity. It seemed way out of Harry's comfort zone. Nola flipped to the front page and saw "Massapequa Public Library" stamped across the first page. Harry didn't really strike her as a library guy. She was pretty sure this was Rafe's as well.

There were also a bunch of pamphlets in Harry's locker talking about European ancestry and how it was being lost to immigrant invaders. A picture of a Confederate flag was taped to the right-hand side of his locker. None of that was surprising.

At the bottom of the locker, she found the remnants of what was probably Harry's lunch from a few weeks ago. Her stomach turning, she closed the locker back up.

Damn it. She didn't have much more to go on. As she relocked his locker, she glanced at the workbench. Molly was gone.

Nola hustled up the stairs and out the door. She wound her way around the halls, back toward the front of the school. The school was quiet. No after-school activities seemed to have been scheduled for today. At least, no official ones. Every once in a while, she would catch a glimpse of some kids in a classroom or in the parking lot.

It all looked so normal, yet a murder had occurred just beyond the soccer field not that long ago. Nola had looked up the details while she'd waited for night to fall at Rafe's apartment. It was similar to another kill by MS-13 at Central Islip High School. Sadly, neither case was unusual for the two school districts. Gang violence, while not at the levels in Tijuana, where Rafe was from, was still incredibly common.

It was strange how people could just get used to the violence that was a part of their life. Nola had gotten used to it herself. Her upbringing hadn't exactly been peaceful. She'd gone to a school not too different from this one. And she'd managed to side-step the violence, at least most of the time.

But not always.

She shook herself from going down that road and pushed herself out of the heavy front doors. Her phone rang just as she stepped into the parking lot. She answered it as she crossed the lot toward her car. "Bishop?"

"Juan Casteel is dead."

Nola paused for only a second, unlocking her door before she nodded and yanked the door open. "I had a feeling it might go that way."

"There were signs of torture. And there was a call to his work cell coming from Riverhead."

Nola settled behind the wheel. "Where in Riverhead?"

"A motel. The Sayonara Motel."

"Sounds like a dump."

"It doesn't even have a webpage, so I'm guessing it is," Bishop replied. "But I think you need to hurry, Nola. I found him awfully quick, and if anybody else was monitoring Casteel's phone . . ."

Nola slammed the car door, putting the key in the ignition. "Then they've found Rafe too."

CHAPTER TEN

RAFE

AFTER SPLASHING cold water on his face, Rafe lifted his head and stared at his reflection in the bathroom mirror, which was scratched and bent at the edges. Something he really didn't want to think about was dried into the corners. His face was framed by all of it. His dark eyes had dark circles underneath them. His cheeks looked hollow. He looked lost.

Which was appropriate, because he was lost. God, how had it come to this? He'd been so proud the day he'd been sworn in as an officer. He'd been raised by his grandmother, who'd instilled in him the importance of helping others and doing what was right. He'd been raised on a farm far outside Mexico City, so he'd been protected in many ways from the violence of the cartels throughout his life. He'd known about their activities and what they were up to, of course. But he'd been so young, so idealistic. He hadn't truly understood how horrific the cartels could be.

And he certainly hadn't understood how far their tentacles could reach into the police department and all aspects of the government. The first introduction to that reach had been his training officer, Alex Ruiz. He'd been on the take. Rafe hadn't understood at first why the officer was cozying up with what he considered to be suspicious individuals.

It didn't take long for the training officer to make the rules clear: Rafe was to keep his mouth shut and his ears and eyes closed when Alex was conducting business.

But his grandmother's lessons had been ingrained in him. The first time he'd been offered a bribe, he'd been on the force for three years. The man had handed it to him with a smirk on his face, confident in Rafe's response. Rafe had him arrested and thrown in jail.

By the time Rafe's shift had ended, his car's tires had been slashed, and the guy was gone, the paperwork as well. Rafe knew then he had to be smarter about how he approached this. So he started taking notes. He started wearing recording devices to make sure that he cataloged everything.

And he didn't tell a soul. Not anyone in his department, not anyone in his family, no one. He didn't know who he could trust. And as for his family, he couldn't risk putting any of them in danger. So over the years, he silently gathered his information and stored it away.

Then, two years ago, he gathered information about the killing of an American agent in Mexico. He filed it away with the rest of it, but he knew that things had changed. With that information, he had an escape route. When the time came that he had to run, he could go to the States with the information and get his family out of Mexico. By then, he had Mariana, Enzo, and Sofia. He knew he couldn't risk their lives, and he didn't know how to bring the cartel to justice while protecting them.

The death of the American, while horrible, offered him a life-line. He just needed to figure out how to take it.

He wasn't sure how he slipped up. He thought maybe it was when he'd first started looking into meeting with the Americans. Or maybe he just hadn't been as good over the previous months of hiding his intelligence collecting. All he knew was that two days after he decided which American office to contact, he was at home for dinner with Mariana and the kids when bullets streaked through the window without warning.

He grabbed Sofia and Enzo and hit the floor. Mariana hadn't been as lucky. Following the bullets were petrol bombs. The front of the house exploded. He grabbed the kids and Mariana's body and pulled them into the root cellar.

The house had burned down around them. The cartel had only stayed long enough to make sure that the entire structure was in flames and that no one escaped. Then they left.

When Rafe emerged from the cellar with his family, his whole life was gone. Mariana was gone. He buried her hastily in the backyard, knowing that he couldn't do anything more official than that. He grabbed the two kids, and with only the clothes on their backs, they started walking for the American border.

He stared at his reflection again. And now, he didn't even have that escape route open to him. He splashed more water on his face, then patted it dry with a rough towel. He glanced at the phone, but that didn't make it ring. Casteel had never taken this long to get back to him before. What was he supposed to do? Where was he supposed to run?

Without a car, there was no way to easily get off Long Island. Public transportation would be monitored, and he didn't have enough money for any other means.

He needed to reach to his handler. He'd seemed on the up and up, but Rafe just didn't know for sure.

Because someone had to have told the cartel where he was.

He was sure those cops had been on the cartel's payroll. That was the only reasonable explanation.

Which meant there was no one in this country that he trusted. There was no one in Mexico that he trusted either. He was on his own except for Sofia and Enzo. And how was he supposed to protect them?

The cartel had tentacles everywhere. They had the money and the weapons to track him down. He needed to find someone that he could trust. But how the hell was he supposed to do that?

CHAPTER ELEVEN

NOLA

NOLA WASTED no time hopping on the Long Island Expressway and heading out to Riverhead. The LIE stretched from the Queens Midtown Tunnel until practically the end of the island at Calverton. It was the main thoroughfare for a large portion of Long Island's residents, especially those commuting.

It was late in the day, and unfortunately those commuters were still on the road. The LIE got congested pretty quick. It wasn't as bad as the Cross Bronx—nothing was as bad as the Cross Bronx—but Nola wasn't exactly cruising along.

She did not miss commuting in this kind of traffic. When she'd switched from CIA agent to analyst, she had commuted to Langley from her and David's home out in Virginia. She'd done it willingly, even though it had been brutal. But it had been for Molly. They'd found a home only twenty minutes away from Ileana. They saw her at least three or four times a week. Hectic as it had been, she would rather be back there than in her current existence.

This time, the trip took about forty-five minutes to reach the Riverhead exit, then she sat in the bumper-to-bumper traffic of cars getting off at the exit. Nola hoped that whoever else was keeping track of Casteel's calls was a little farther away.

She passed the entrance to the parking lot for the outlet mall and left most of the traffic behind. The lot was packed with people desperate to get their shopping on.

Nola couldn't remember the last time she'd shopped for fun. She wasn't sure she had *ever* actually shopped for fun.

But as soon as she had the thought, she knew that wasn't right. Shopping for Molly had always been fun. Nola hadn't had the pink dresses and little bows when she was little, and so she made sure that Molly had all of that.

She made a left a mile past the outlets. The Sayonara Motel was another half mile down the road. This was the less-developed portion of Riverhead, a light-year away from the bright lights of the outlet mall development and the restaurants and businesses that had sprung up around it.

Nola drove down a street where most of the buildings were shuttered for the night, even though it wasn't yet six. Ahead, she saw the lit-up sign for the Sayonara Motel. The motel sign had been modeled after what she thought was supposed to be Japanese writing. It really looked more like a bad Chinese restaurant font. She wasn't sure if the original owners were of Japanese ancestry or if this was a horrible example of 1970s exploitation. She was thinking it was probably the latter.

The hotel itself was white with black trim and red doors. It looked like it hadn't been painted in a few decades. A woman stumbled across the street in a dress that could barely be categorized as one.

Two guys in their twenties sat on the tailgate of a pickup,

sharing a bottle and watching her.

None of them was a ringing endorsement for the motel's clientele.

Nola thought about and then immediately discounted pulling into the parking lot. The parking lot only had one exit and was completely surrounded by the motel on three and a half sides. If she went in there, she'd be stuck. It would be a shooting gallery for anyone who got the higher ground.

She went down the block, turned around, and pulled up on the opposite side of the street, which hopefully would allow her to make a quick getaway if necessary.

She glanced around the neighborhood and saw more than a few people out for a walk, which meant she couldn't get suited up at the back of her truck. Too many eyes. She reached into the backseat and pulled the black duffel onto the passenger seat.

She pulled off her jacket and then pulled on the bulletproof vest. It was awkward trying to get it on while sitting behind the steering wheel, but she eventually managed it. After slipping her jacket on over it, she zipped it up to keep the vest hidden. No need to announce her intention.

She slipped knives into holders on the side of her pants and then tucked her gun into the back of her waistband. She slipped a few extra magazines into her pockets, zipping them up. She zipped the bag back up and put it on the ground in the back of the car. Enzo and Sofia's stuffed animals lay on the seat, on their sides. She stepped out of the car and pocketed the keys.

Everything was quiet. No sign of any issues.

She smiled. That was good. It meant that she was the first one here. Which meant that—

A car peeled down the road and sped into the motel parking lot. As the car passed, light splashed across the faces of the two front occupants. Both had extensive face tattoos.

The hallmarks of MS-13.

CHAPTER TWELVE

RAFE

TAKING A DEEP BREATH, Rafe stared at himself in the mirror and forced a smile to his face. He could hear the strains of the kids' TV show through the bathroom door. He needed to at least try and pretend everything was normal so as not to worry them too much. His smile in the mirror looked a little maniacal to him, but it was the best he could manage at the moment. He opened the bathroom door, clapping his hands. "Okay, you two, who's hungry now?"

"I am!" Sofia said, jumping up and down on the bed. Next to her, Enzo looked up, his eyes bright with a smile on his face as he nodded.

"Okay. There's a vending machine right down the parking lot. How about if we have a candy dinner?"

"Really?" Sofia asked.

Rafe nodded. "Why not? We'll treat this as a little vacation."

"Yes!" Sofia scrambled off the bed.

Rafe's heart lifted at her joy, even though part of him cringed at the fact that he could only afford to provide them with candy for dinner. But he wasn't going to focus on that now. When the kids were asleep, he would figure some stuff out. Right now, his job was to make sure that they thought life was as normal as possible.

A shadow passed in front of the window. Rafe's breath went still. Sofia skipped toward the door. He grabbed her by the shoulder and pulled her back. "Wait."

The door burst open.

Two men heavily tattooed across their chests and even up their faces burst into the room, machetes in their right hands.

Rafe grabbed a screaming Sofia and pushed her toward Enzo as the first man rushed toward him. Rafe slammed his foot into the man's chest. He went flying back as the second one came at him almost at the same time.

Rafe slipped to the side, the blade just missing his shoulder. He grabbed ahold of the man's wrist and brought the blade back to the man's calf, slicing as he passed. He slammed the side of his left hand into the man's elbow, forcing the arm to bend, then whipped the arm along the side. He brought the machete up along the man's back and impaled it there. The man screamed. Rafe pushed him toward his friend, who was getting to his feet.

"Sofia, Enzo, run!"

He grabbed ahold of the first man who rushed him and shoved him up against the wall. Sofia grabbed Enzo and ran for the door. But a third man stepped into the doorway, blocking their escape.

CHAPTER THIRTEEN

NOLA

THE CAR with the MS-13 members barreled into the Sayonara Motel. By the time Nola sprinted across the road and into the parking lot, the car had stopped in the middle of the parking lot, facing the entrance. Three doors were thrown wide. The driver remained behind the wheel. The men bolted from it to a door two from the end. One man kicked in the door and another one followed him in. The third stood right outside the door.

Nola could see into part of the room as she sprinted into the parking lot. She kept an eye on the driver in case he pulled a gun, but his attention was on the room as well.

The man at the door had his back to her as he stood in the doorway. Beyond him, Nola heard Rafael Ortiz yell out, "Sofia, Enzo, run!"

Nola had her Browning out, but the man at the doorway blocked her view into the room. She couldn't get a good idea of where the children were. She couldn't risk shooting him and having the bullet go into the room and hit one of the kids.

Damn it. She holstered the weapon and picked up her speed. She darted around the car and came up on the sidewalk outside the motel room.

The man in the doorway turned, hearing her approach. She leapt, her side kick landing in the middle of his chest. He flew back into the doorframe, slamming his head on the wood.

Nola grabbed his face. Her fingers plunged into his eye sockets as she slammed his head back into the doorway and then wrenched him forward before he collapsed on the sidewalk. He reached for his face with a scream as she kicked him in the head. Sofia and Enzo darted out of the hotel room and into the parking lot. A fourth gang member stepped from the car.

Luckily, he wasn't blocking the kids from her shot. She pulled her weapon and fired off three shots. He dropped to his knees and then went face down on the parking lot floor.

A second car screeched into the parking lot. It barreled toward the two kids.

"Sofia! Enzo! To me!" she yelled as she sprinted across the parking lot.

Sofia stuttered to a halt. She grabbed Enzo's arm, looking at the racing car and then back toward Nola. She yanked Enzo with her and started to run back toward Nola.

Nola emptied to her weapon into the driver's side of the car. The driver lost control and slammed into a parked car. A man stumbled from the passenger side.

Nola was already there.

She kicked the door. It caught the man on his chin and neck, and he let out a scream. Nola grabbed him by the top of his head, spun him around, and slammed him back face first into the edge of the doorframe. He dropped to the ground. Nola stepped back. The passenger was moaning, but he wasn't going to be going after anyone anytime soon. And the driver was definitely gone.

Her heart raced, and her mouth felt dry. She scanned the parking lot. Rafael stumbled from the motel room, his arm bloody.

"Papa!" Sofia rushed across the parking lot toward him.

Nola hurried over to them. Rafael's head jerked up. He pulled the kids behind him as she approached. She raised her hands, blanching as she realized blood was still on one from when she'd treated one of the gang members' heads as a bowling ball. "Not an enemy."

Sofia tugged on her father's shirt. "She fought the bad men, Papa."

"Who are you?" Rafe demanded.

"I was asked to come find you, sent by people connected with the United States government."

"Are you an agent?"

Nola shook her head. "Former. Now I just kind of do my own thing. I was asked to get you to safety."

Rafe studied her, his dark eyes full of concern and suspicion. She couldn't blame him. He and his family had been through hell, and that was before this debacle.

"Look, the cops are on their way," she said. "There are a lot of things this type of motel will ignore, but six bodies is not one of them. I know right now you don't know who to trust, and I'm not saying trust me forever. But how about you trust me to at least get you away from this situation?"

Rafael's eyes bored into her. "If you do anything to harm me or my children, I will kill you."

There was conviction in the man's face and a desire to keep his family safe, no matter the cost. She nodded, understanding the sentiment perfectly. "As well you should."

CHAPTER FOURTEEN

RAFE

RESIDENTS of the Sayonara Motel were starting to stir. A few curtains shifted from windows. On the opposite side of the parking lot, a door cracked open, a head popping out before disappearing again.

The woman was right. They needed to move. He studied her as she stood across from him. She was about 5'8" with dark-blonde hair and green eyes. She wore a leather jacket and jeans with heavy-duty boots. Even with such clothes, it was clear that she was strong and muscular.

And from the way she'd taken out the last three of the MS-13 guys, it was also clear that she was trained. She hadn't made any moves toward him, but that could just mean that she was smart and not trying to tip him off.

His mind ran in circles, trying to figure out what he was supposed to do here. He didn't know her, but she had protected the kids from those gang members. The cartel could have hired her. But of course, if that was the case, she probably would've just killed them already.

A woman in a pink silk kimono at the end of the hall stuck her head around the doorway and let out a little small cry, then ducked back in, her phone at her ear.

"We really need to go," the woman said.

The woman stood across from him, her hands still up, not making any move to leave, but he felt her urgency. The cops would be here at any moment. He nodded. "Do you have a car?"

She nodded toward the street. "Out there."

He took Sofia and Enzo's hands and started walking. The woman fell in step with them, glancing around and watching as they walked.

Definitely trained.

And if she was on their side, well, then that could be a very good thing. But if she wasn't . . .

The woman led them across the street to an old Bronco. She unlocked it, pulled out a black duffel bag, then moved to the back of the car. Rafael watched her. She opened the tailgate. Dropping the black bag, she pulled out a small navy-blue bag.

Rafe stood at the open side door, uncertain.

"Bella!" Sofia cried, scrambling in. She lunged into the car, grabbing the bunny she'd had since birth. "Look, Enzo, Alma!" She held up the stuffed dog that Enzo had since his birth.

Rafael picked up Enzo and placed him in the backseat, quickly putting on Enzo's seatbelt. "Sofia, put on your seatbelt."

The woman had the car started by the time he closed the passenger door. She had pulled a bag of wipes from somewhere and was cleaning the blood from her hands.

He squirmed, and a jolt of pain ran through his side. The woman rummaged through the bag and pulled out a towel. "For your arm."

He took it with a nod of thanks. He didn't think she'd even noticed the wound. He pressed the towel to his arm, trying not to make any noises as a second jolt of pain lanced up his side. He'd gotten distracted when the third member had shown up in the doorway. Just that one moment of inattention had allowed the other guy to slice him along the bicep.

The guy from the door had disappeared in a flash of movement. The kids bolted, and Rafe had finished with his guy before stumbling to the doorway. He'd gotten there in time to see the woman shoot out the driver's window of the car aiming for Sofia and Enzo. And then he'd watched as she skillfully took down the remaining attacker. She was fearless. She was strong. And she was lethal.

Rafe glanced into the back of the car. Both kids clutched their stuffed animals to their chests. They'd moved as close to each other as the seatbelts would allow. Sofia held Enzo's hand in hers, her other hand protectively wrapped around Bella.

The sight of Bella and Alma in Enzo and Sofia's arms warmed his heart. They were something familiar, something the kids loved. That was what they needed.

But both kids were shaking, their eyes glassy. He knew they were going into shock. The woman handed him the bag. "There's a blanket in there for the kids."

He unzipped it as she pulled away from the curb. He pulled the blanket out and, reaching over the seat, tucked it around both of them.

"Daddy, are the bad men gone now?" Sofia asked, her voice whisper soft.

"Yes, baby. They're gone."

Sofia nodded. "Will they be back?"

He wanted to tell her they wouldn't be. That she was safe. But he couldn't bring himself to lie. "It's okay for now."

She looked into his eyes, recognizing he hadn't answered her question. She nodded and then turned her gaze to the window.

Rafe's heart clutched. *Damn it.*

He turned back to the front, watching the woman from the corner of his eye. She had grabbed their stuffed animals. Was it just a nice thing to do? Or part of a manipulation?

He shook his head. God, he hated thinking like this. When he was younger, he trusted people. Probably because those people had proven worthy of it. But now he didn't know who to have faith in. In Mexico, he'd seen friends stab one another in the back just for a bigger paycheck. He'd seen family members take each other down in the name of loyalty to a gang that would turn on them as quickly as they had turned on their family.

The woman drove quickly down the street. Rafe grabbed his seatbelt. He winced as he crushed his arm along the door. "What's your name?"

"Nola, Nola James. And you're Rafael Ortiz, of the Tijuana Police Department."

Rafe started but then realized it was silly. Of course she knew his name. "You can call me Rafe."

"Okay, Rafe. Let's get you and your family somewhere safe."

Nola quickly made a right at the light and headed away from the motel. A flash of police lights appeared in the distance. Making a left, Nola flicked a glance in the rearview mirror as the police car crossed the intersection, heading for the motel. "We're good," she said.

"Are we? Because I thought we were good at that hotel."

"You were for a little bit. But MS-13 has a long reach."

Rafe glanced toward the back of the car. Enzo now had his head down in Sofia's lap. Sofia looked out the window, lost in thought. He lowered his voice. "The cartel does as well. We can't go anywhere where there are cameras."

Nola turned onto LIE heading west. "I know a place. No cameras. No public allowed. It will be safe."

"No place is truly safe," Rafe said.

Nola turned toward him and met his gaze. She gave him a nod, acknowledging the point.

And somehow that little nod of acknowledgment made him feel better. Nola was more than a little paranoid herself, it seemed.

But then he wondered what in her past had made her like that. The old him hoped whatever was in her past wasn't as bad as what was in his. But the new him hoped it was and that it had prepared her to do whatever was necessary to keep his family safe.

CHAPTER FIFTEEN

NOLA

THEY GOT a small break on the LIE. It wasn't too busy. Most people were heading east rather than west toward the city. It was only a twenty-minute drive from Riverhead to the exit for Wading River. Part of her wondered if she should get them a little farther away. But right now, she had nothing planned. And she needed to suss things out a little bit to make sure that she had a safe exit strategy for the Ortiz family. Which meant that right now she needed a safe base from which to plan.

Rafe sat in the passenger seat, staring out the window. Nola watched him from the corner of her eye as she drove. He was a tough man. And obviously a man who loved his children.

Nola placed a lot of faith in her gut instincts. Over the years, she'd trained herself to read body language, tone, and an array of other factors. And all that experience told her Rafe Ortiz was what he seemed: a desperate father looking to protect his family.

She wasn't fully sold on it because she'd been burned before. But she'd be incredibly surprised if Rafe wasn't who he seemed.

She flicked another glance in the rearview mirror. Sofia and Enzo were curled up in the backseat. Molly sat on the other side of Enzo. She looked up at Nola. "You need to help them, Mommy."

Nola gave her a nod and then turned her attention back to the road. The car remained quiet for the rest of the twenty-minute ride. The Ortiz family had all drifted off, even Rafe. He'd been living on a razor's edge all day, so she wasn't surprised. That adrenaline drop could be pretty substantial.

"Rafe," she said softly as they approached the exit.

He started in his seat, jolting up. His head jerked toward Nola.

"It's okay. I just wanted to let you know that we're getting close."

He rubbed his face with his good arm. He winced as he brushed the other arm against the door.

"When we get there, we'll have to take a look at that arm."

"It's fine. Where exactly is 'there'?"

"A friend of mine runs a camp for at-risk youth. It's tucked away. Some of the kids are former gang members, so they have strong security and a long fence to keep everybody inside."

"Gang members? We can't go—"

Nola cut him off. "The kids inside didn't want to be gang members. They were forced into it. Darrin keeps them safe. He gives them a chance to grow up and a chance to be kids. He's got a school on site, and most of them go on to college afterward or to apprenticeships. But he doesn't send any of them to places where they may be pulled back into gang activity. He runs a tight ship. And he's a good man."

Nola could tell that Rafe was worried. But Darrin's camp was the best place for them right now. It was set in the back and beyond.

No one headed down that road unless they were going to the camp. Even then, it was two miles down the road. Someone who was lost would turn around well before then. And anyone who didn't, the camp would know about it well before they reached the gate.

She turned onto the road leading to the camp, and the car began to buck and move on the gravel road.

"Daddy? Where are we?" Sofia asked from the backseat.

"We're going to a friend of Nola's."

"Is it safe?" Sofia asked.

Nola's heart broke a little at the question. An eight-year-old shouldn't have to worry if she was safe.

Of course, Molly hadn't known that she was in danger. Would it have been better if she'd known?

Enzo stirred as well from the backseat. He sat up, rubbing his eyes. He had his father's eyes while Sofia looked more like her mother.

Enzo reached out for Sofia's hand. Sofia immediately grabbed it and tucked it into her lap. They were close, those two. Nola supposed they had to be.

No one spoke for the short ride to the camp entrance. When Nola pulled up to it, there was one guard on duty at the guard shack. He stepped outside and walked up to the truck. "I'm sorry. This is private property."

"I'm a friend of Darrin's. Tell him Nola James is here."

The guard paused for just a moment and then nodded, stepping back into the guard shack. He made a call from the phone inside.

When he stepped back outside, he held up his iPad. A man with long dark braids pulled back in a low ponytail was on the screen. He had dark eyes set in a face with smooth dark skin. Only the wrinkles around his eyes showed his age. He grinned when he caught sight of Nola. "It *is* you! Come on in."

The guard pushed a button, and the gate swung open. Nola drove slowly down the dirt drive toward the main house.

Darrin's camp sat on forty-five acres. It was an old summer camp that he'd had refurbished. They passed half a dozen small cottages on the way in. Security lights highlighted a pool in the distance and a large playground. The pool was covered over, but Sofia and Enzo's eyes lit up at the sight of the playground next to it.

"Dad, can we play on the swings?" Sofia asked.

"Maybe later, sweetheart," Rafe said.

Nola pulled to a stop in front of the main house. It was a long single-story log cabin. The bright-green door opened up, and Darrin Johnson stepped through. He smiled wide as Nola turned the car off. Nola couldn't help but smile back at the sight of him. Darrin's good nature was infectious.

He crossed the porch and headed down the stairs as Nola stepped out.

"Nola!" Darrin held out his arms. Nola walked over to him and let him hug her. Darrin was one of the few people that hugged her. There just didn't seem to be a way to avoid it. Most people accepted that Nola was stepping back from the world—Darrin didn't.

Or maybe he didn't know.

Darrin backed up and looked into Nola's face. "I'm sorry. I heard what happened."

Nola nodded at him, her whole body feeling tight.

Darrin, recognizing the pain he unintentionally caused, quickly switched gears. "But it's good to see you. And I see you brought us some guests."

Rafe had stepped out of the car.

"Yes, this is Mr. Ralph Smith and his two children, Sofia and Enzo."

Darrin zeroed in on Rafe's arm. "It looks like you could use some help, my friend."

Sofia climbed out of Rafe's car door behind him. She peered out from behind her father.

Darrin smiled. "And you must be Sofia. Welcome."

The kids both still looked scared. Nola placed a hand on her belly. "Well, I don't know about anyone else, but I'm starving. Any chance there's still some dinner hanging around?"

Darrin patted his round stomach. "You know there's always food at my place. Come on in. We'll get everyone settled."

CHAPTER SIXTEEN

RAFE

THE CAMP WAS DEFINITELY off the beaten track; Rafe had to admit that. In the dark, it looked like something out of an American horror film, but Rafe tried to shake those images away as he helped Enzo out of the car. Darrin seemed a friendly sort, but Rafe had seen the tattoos. He knew that in his earlier days, Darrin had been up to no good. But from what Nola said, it looked like he turned his life around.

Darrin led them inside. The main house had wide wooden plank floors. The furniture was all utilitarian but comfortable. There was a green couch and two matching chairs, all with heavy wooden frames. Photos and hand-drawn pictures dotted the walls. And in the corner stood a stuffed seven-foot black bear.

But what really drew Rafe's attention the most was the smell of food. His stomach grumbled in response. It had been a long day, and he hadn't eaten a thing.

"Why don't you guys make yourself comfortable?" Darrin indicated a heavy dark wooden table and chairs on the far side of the room. There was an open kitchen right next to it with a white counter in between the kitchen and the table.

Darrin disappeared inside, and Nola followed him.

The kids stayed near Rafe as he wandered over to a wall of photos. Darrin was in almost all of them. They started when he was maybe about thirty until now, when he had to be close to sixty. In each shot, he stood with different kids. All kids from the camp over the years.

There were more than a dozen of him standing happily next to someone in graduation gear. Another wall was covered with the awards he'd received from different community groups for his work with at-risk youth. It looked like Darrin had done a lot of good in this world.

Sofia and Enzo had walked to the far side of the room and were standing in front of the giant bear, staring up at it. Its mouth was open, its arms extended forward. Enzo shifted closer to Sofia.

Rafe smiled. "It's stuffed. It can't hurt you. Go ahead, touch it."

Sofia glanced over at Rafe and then reached out a tentative hand toward the bear. She smiled and encouraged Enzo to do the same. He shook his head.

Rafe sighed, not sure what to do about his son's increasing nervousness. The situation today certainly hadn't helped. Through the kitchen pass-through, Nola and Darrin spoke quietly but with familiarity as they put food together. It was clear the two cared about one another.

Rafe walked over to them. "Is there a bathroom nearby? I'd like to get the kids cleaned up."

"Of course, of course. Down the hall, second on the right." Darrin pointed at the hall across from the front door.

"Thanks. Come on, you two. Let's get cleaned up before you eat."

The two of them hurried over to him, and they made their way down the hall. They passed a bedroom on the left and a study on the right, followed by the bathroom with red walls next to it. They all squeezed in, and Rafe helped them get cleaned up.

By the time they got back to the kitchen area, platters of food had been laid out on the table. Sofia gave a little gasp as she saw them. There was chicken, guacamole, cheese, peppers, onions, and everything needed to make some good tacos.

Darrin placed some salsa and sour cream on the table. "Sorry it's not fresh. But I promise it's good. Sean's a great cook."

"Sean's his boyfriend," Nola said.

"He's not my boyfriend, not exactly," Darrin mumbled.

Nola smiled at him. The smile changed her whole face. For a moment, she looked carefree. She looked beautiful. Rafe was struck by the difference. But then, as soon as the moment of lightness appeared, it disappeared from her face. She nodded toward Rafe's arm. "We really need to look at that."

"Let me get the kids some plates, and then I'll—"

Darrin waved them away. "I can get them set up. I've been making plates for kids for years."

Rafe looked at Sofia and Enzo. "Will you two be okay for a minute? I'll be right down the hall in the bathroom."

Sofia nodded, her eyes still on the food. "We'll be fine, Papa."

Enzo darted a glance at him. There was still too much fear in Enzo's eyes for Rafe's liking. Rafe leaned down. "I'll be right down the hall. Not far at all, okay?"

Enzo nodded.

Rafe leaned over and kissed him on the forehead. "Good boy."

He stood and followed Nola down the hallway. By the time

he reached the bathroom, she'd arranged the first-aid kit on the sink.

She looked up as he stepped in. The bathroom felt warmer all of a sudden, and he realized just how small it was.

He swallowed as his heart started to race. *It's nothing. I just haven't been this close to an attractive woman since Mariana.*

CHAPTER SEVENTEEN

NOLA

A FEW MINUTES AGO, when Nola had stepped into the kitchen with Darrin, he had asked her questions about Rafe and his kids. But she didn't want to provide him with too much information for a multitude of reasons, not the least of which was keeping Darrin safe. The less he knew, the better for him. So all she told him was that Rafe and his family needed a safe place and that there were people out there looking for them.

Darrin looked into Nola's eyes. "Is he a good person?"

Nola had paused to consider the question. From what she'd read, he appeared to be, but she couldn't swear by it. "I think so."

Darrin nodded. "Okay, then. Let's get them fed."

Now Nola stood in Darrin's small bathroom, the first-aid kit displayed in front of her. Rafe appeared in the doorway. He took up the whole space. She hadn't realized how big he was before.

He had to top out at about 6'3". And he had wide shoulders. She nodded at him. "Let's see what we've got."

Rafe stepped closer to her as Nola pulled out some scissors. She moved to start cutting the sleeve.

"Hold on."

Rafe started to take the shirt off. Nola helped him as he struggled over the cut. Rafe tossed the shirt to the floor.

Nola focused on the wound on his arm but not before getting an eyeful of strong pectoral muscles and a six-pack stomach. Apparently exercise had been part of the routine these last few months.

The cut had stopped bleeding, which was good, but it was nasty and deep. She peered at it with a frown. "I think this is going to need a couple of stitches."

"Do you know how to do that?"

Nola had stitched herself up so many times that she'd lost count at this point. "Yes."

She pulled out the needle and thread, laying it on the counter, and then got some of the peroxide out. She paused as she placed some on a cotton swab. "This is going to sting."

Rafe gripped the edge of the counter. "Go ahead."

Nola didn't hesitate.

Rafe sucked in a breath and then blew it out when she was done.

She took out the numbing cream and spread it around the cut. "We just need to wait a minute for that to take effect."

"Do you do this a lot? Save people you don't know?"

Nola shrugged, meeting his gaze in the mirror. "Some." She nodded down the hall. "How are the kids?"

"I don't know. I don't think it's really hit them, everything that's happened. But it will later."

Nola nodded. "Your son doesn't seem to talk much."

Rafe shook his head, his eyes looking haunted in the mirror. "Not since his mother died," he said softly.

Nola felt a moment of kinship with the young boy. She had been changed by the deaths in her life as well. Nola tapped on the skin around Rafe's cut. "How's that?"

"It's good. Go ahead."

She grabbed the needle and inserted it into the skin, pausing to see if he responded. But he didn't even flinch. She continued sewing, stitch after stitch.

"So what's the plan?" Rafe asked. "How long are we staying here?"

"I need to contact some people."

Rafe's head jerked up.

Nola winced, checking his skin to make sure she hadn't just ripped it. "It's okay. They're trustworthy. But I need to see how we can take you in, and safely. Your handler was killed. Until we know that that was unrelated to what's happening to you, we can't trust anyone in that office."

Rafe turned his head quickly toward her, shock splashed across his face. "Juan's dead?"

Nola nodded, tapping him on the arm. He let out a breath, trying to relax his arm.

"Yes. He was missing all morning. Then they found his body. It wasn't a good scene."

"Torture?"

Nola nodded. "Working assumption is that the cartel got to him."

"To get to me," Rafe said softly.

Nola nodded. "That's what they figure, although he has a few other cases. It's possible it's related to one of them."

"But you don't buy that. It's too much of a coincidence that someone came after me at the same time that someone went after him."

Nola nodded. "Yeah."

Rafe dropped his head, shaking it before looking up at Nola. He looked completely lost, completely powerless. Like life was batting him around like a cat with a toy. And right now it was.

"Hey, we'll figure this out. We'll find a way to get you and your family safe." She reached out and touched him on the shoulder. His warmth spread through her hand. She yanked it back, the feeling curling up in her, and it was not at all what she expected.

She turned her attention back to the first-aid kit and quickly pulled out a bandage and some Steri-Strips. She covered the stitches. "Try to keep it clean. If you grab a shower later, just make sure that you don't get that side wet, okay?"

Rafe nodded as he straightened. And suddenly the bathroom seemed awfully small.

He looked down at Nola. "Thank you, Nola."

She gave him an abrupt nod. He turned and stepped out of the room.

Nola let out a breath, her hands feeling a little shaky. She shook her head. *Nope. Nope, nope, nope.*

CHAPTER EIGHTEEN

RAFE

AT DINNER, Sofia and Enzo filled their stomachs. Rafe had been happy to see it. He, too, had eaten his fill. He'd tried to take a little less, but Darrin had insisted he eat more.

Now, the fire cast a dim glow over the living room. Sofia and Enzo had curled up on the couch and fallen asleep while the adults tidied up the food.

When the dishes were put away, Nola said, "I'm going to go do a perimeter sweep. I'll be back."

She stopped next to Rafe as he placed a blanket over Sofia and Enzo. As he straightened, she handed him a picture.

"I found this in your locker. Thought you might want it back."

The picture was from two years ago. They'd gone on a one-week vacation to the coast. It had been glorious.

And the picture was the only one he had of Mariana. He took it from Nola, a lump forming in his throat. "Thank you."

She gave him a nod and headed for the door.

Rafe watched her go, wondering about who she was. She had brought his children their favorite toys and him the last photo he had of them as a family. Yet he'd seen her in action. She was lethal. Heart and violence: it was a perplexing combination.

He knew there was something there, behind her actions. He'd seen moments of levity in her, but it was almost like she felt guilty for even having them. Which meant there was pain in her past. He had no doubt it was what had formed the woman she was today.

Because he felt guilty for the same thing.

Walking across the room, Darrin nodded toward the two chairs by the fireplace. "Come join me."

Rafe sank into a chair as Darrin stepped over to a small table with a decanter and three glasses. He poured a dark liquid into two and handed one to Rafe before taking a seat next to him.

Rafe took a sip. Scotch. He grimaced. He was not a huge fan. But today he could definitely use something stronger than water. He took another sip.

Darrin settled into the chair next to him. They sat in companionable silence, sipping on their drinks. Rafe let himself take a moment to relax and let go. At this exact moment in time, everyone was safe. He couldn't guarantee the next moment or the one after that, but right at this moment, he could let himself release the terror that had such a tight hold on him.

Darrin broke the silence. "Nola's a good woman. She's fierce, protective of those that deserve it. Did she tell you how we met?"

"She doesn't seem to talk much, especially about herself."

Darrin nodded with a smile. "That's always been true, but especially these last two years. But that's her story to tell. *My* story is how the two of us met." Darrin settled back. "It was nine years ago. Nola was a CIA agent. At least, I think it was the CIA she worked for. She never officially said. Anyway, one of my kids had left the camp. He went back home. He got into some trouble, got grabbed, and pulled back down to Mexico. Him and his sister both."

Darrin shook his head. "It was a bad scene. I didn't know what to do, where to go, or who to ask for help. Everybody I talked to in the State Department just told me that there was nothing they could do.

"And then, three weeks later, Nola showed up. She had Scott and Alicia with her. She brought them back here. She'd done her research on me and knew that they would be safe.

"Then she went after the men who took them. Not the foot soldiers, the *bosses*. I read in the newspaper about the bodies found in a warehouse, all gang related. A rival gang had been blamed, but I knew the truth.

"Nola showed up again a few days later. Once again, she wasn't empty-handed. She had a girl with her, only twelve years old. She'd been used as bait by the gang. But her home life wasn't something any child should return to. So Nola brought her here to me. And then Nola stayed for a little while because the girl asked her to. Because the girl was scared. That little girl is now in her last year at SUNY Stony Brook. She's pre-med."

Darrin smiled, and Rafe recognized that smile. It was a father's pride.

"After that, Nola stopped by every now and then to check on the three children, make sure they were all right. And sometimes just to say hello. But all that came to a stop two years ago."

Darrin's face clouded. "She is a rare woman, Nola. She's like a guardian from old. She believes in right and wrong. She doesn't believe that just because you're stronger you get to do whatever you want. I know of three lives she's saved, and I doubt that's the end of her heroism. What I'm trying to say is, I don't know what trouble you're in, but if Nola is on your side, then things just got a whole lot better for you."

Rafe studied the man's profile. He looked older in the firelight. His words held the conviction of a convert. He was firmly on Team Nola.

And Rafe hoped that he was right in his assessment of her. Because he desperately needed someone like that to be on his side.

CHAPTER NINETEEN

NOLA

THE CAMP WAS quiet as Nola made her way around the cabins. There were twenty-four kids, ranging in age from eleven to twenty, living at the camp. Most had come from violent backgrounds. Darrin's camp was their refuge from a cold, uncaring world. Nola knew how important that kind of refuge could be to a child.

She made her way to the security office. It was a small building just inside the main gate. She knocked on the door.

"Come in," came the voice from inside.

Nola stepped into the room. It was very basic—four screens lined up along an eight-foot table constantly scrolled through different camera angles across the camp. It might have looked no frills, but all of Darrin's security had been through the police academy and were well trained in weapons, hand to hand, and surveillance. They just didn't have a lot of bells and whistles. All the money went back into the camp and to the paychecks of Darrin's staff.

A man in his early thirties stood up from behind the table. He was about five eight and had a strong muscular build. His tattoo sleeves were displayed below his rolled-up shirt sleeves. He smiled. "Hi, I'm Toine, short for Antoine. Darrin told me you would be stopping by."

Nola shook his hand. "Nola James."

Toine's mouth fell open. "Wait, you're Nola James? Scott and Alicia's Nola James?"

Nola grimaced. "I suppose so."

Toine's face broke into a huge smile. "Scott's going to be so mad when I tell him you were here and he didn't get to see you. Alicia too. This is her last year of law school. Scott's wife's pregnant. It's their first. He was just telling me the other day the name's going to be Nola if it's a girl and James if it's a boy."

Nola's mouth fell open. She had absolutely no idea what to say to that. "I . . . uh, that's something."

Toine chuckled. "Scott said you'd probably hate it. But he wants his baby to know about his guardian angel."

Nola felt distinctly uncomfortable at Toine's words and at the same time, touched. "Tell him . . . tell him I said congratulations."

"I will. Now, I'm guessing you want to see the security layout?"

Nola nodded. "Yeah. I'd appreciate it."

"No problem." Toine waved her over to the screens and explained where each of the cameras were, the guard rotation, and the basic security precautions. "We haven't had any problems in about the last year."

"And before that?"

Toine cracked his knuckles. "Guy came in from LA. Thought he was going to get his cousin out, with or without his cousin's consent. We taught him otherwise."

Nola couldn't help but smile. "So where is the guy now?"

"Rikers. He'll be there for another three because he brought an unlicensed firearm with him."

"And his cousin?"

"Going to work out in Oregon this summer. Kid's really got a way with cars. Darrin knows a guy."

Darrin always knew a guy. "Well, thanks for showing me around. I'm going to take a tour of the grounds."

"I'd expect no less." Toine extended his hand. "It's been a real pleasure meeting you, Nola."

"You too, Toine." Nola stepped back outside, feeling a little lighter. She pictured Scott and Alicia when she'd first met them. Thrown in a trunk and dragged back across the border. They'd been held for four days when she caught up with them. They were exhausted, dirty, starving, and completely, utterly terrified.

And now Alicia was about to become a lawyer, and Scott had a baby on the way. She smiled. Not bad.

She walked around the perimeter, checking the gates to make sure that everything was locked up tight. But she found no problems. Darrin ran a tight ship. He was an easygoing man, and an amiable one, but he took no chances when it came to the protection of his kids.

Most of his security force had been former residents here as well. They still lived in some cabins on the far side of the camp. Darrin had created this large extended family for all of them, providing a life to people who only had a nightmare to look forward to before.

Most of the kids here didn't have parents or had parents who should never have been given that title. Sofia and Enzo didn't fit into either of those categories. They had a father who loved them, that was clear. He was also a father who was unable to keep danger from them.

Nola pulled out her phone and dialed Bishop.

Bishop answered quickly. "Nola. I read about the shoot-out. I'm assuming that was you?"

"It was. MS-13 found Rafe and his family. I got them somewhere safe."

Bishop didn't ask where. She didn't need to. She knew almost all of Nola hidey-holes.

"What's going on with the Casteel investigation?"

"They're following their tails trying to figure out what happened to him. They believe it's the cartel, but it's going to take a little bit of time to get them to fine-tune it and to hand off all of his cases."

"I can't keep Rafe and his family here for too long." She didn't want to endanger Darrin or any of his kids. Plus, the longer they stayed in one place, the greater chance of someone discovering them.

"I know. Ileana has interceded with State. She hopes to have the case assigned to someone by tomorrow. And then a new handler. They should be able to create a safehouse for Rafe and his kids."

That was good.

A breeze blew up, bringing with it a chill of cold air. Nola didn't say anything, just stood staring at the trees, a slip of white disappearing into a shadow.

"You okay, Nola?"

Nola was about to give her standard response when words she hadn't intended to say slipped out. "Rafe's daughter is eight years old."

Bishop's voice was heavy with shared pain. "I know. She looks a little bit like her, with the dark hair."

Nola nodded, the lump in her throat making it difficult to speak. She knew Sofia wasn't Molly. Besides the dark hair, they didn't look alike. But it was still hard.

She shook her head as if she could chase away the punch of

grief. She took a deep breath, centering herself. No, Molly was dead. Nola couldn't help her anymore. But she could help Sofia. Sofia was supposed to have died back at her family's home. They all were. Now it was Nola's job to make sure they stayed alive.

Taking another shaky breath, she pulled the emotions back. Acknowledging them was necessary. Addressing them was necessary. And now that she had, she could store them away.

With all the others.

She cleared her throat. "Okay. Let me know if you find anything else."

"I will. And, Nola, if you need anything, call me, okay?"

"Yeah. Thanks, Bishop."

Nola slipped the phone into her back pocket. She stared up at the sky, rolling her shoulders. A heavy weight had settled in her chest ever since she'd seen Rafe's kids. In the last two years, she hadn't worked cases with kids this age. The closest had been Anna Mae's little brother. But he hadn't constantly been with her. This was different. It was tougher than she thought it was going to be.

"They need your help, Mommy."

Nola turned around and smiled as Molly appeared from between the trees. "Hey, sweetheart."

"They're sad. They miss their mommy."

"I know."

"And they're scared too. But you make them feel safer."

"That's good. Do you want to take a walk?"

Molly smiled. "Always."

Nola turned, and Molly fell in step next to her. The ache in her throat grew. More than anything, she wanted to reach out and take Molly's hand, but she knew if she did, the illusion that Molly was still with her would disappear. So she kept her hands firmly behind her back as she walked through the woods with her daughter.

CHAPTER TWENTY

NOLA

THE LIGHTS in the main house had been dimmed by the time Nola finished her walk of the perimeter. The camp was locked up tight. Nola had given the kids from the cabins a wide berth, not wanting to frighten any of them.

The only kid she'd seen was Molly, who kept her company for almost the entire walk. She disappeared just before Nola stepped into the arc of lights by the main cabin.

Nola's heart ached again at Molly's disappearance. Not for the first time, she wondered if these visits were making it easier or harder for her to accept that Molly was gone.

She climbed the stairs and opened the door quietly. Darrin looked up from his seat by the fire and then slowly got to his feet. Nola looked around but didn't spy Rafe or the kids anywhere.

Keeping his voice low, Darrin walked over to her. "I gave

them the guest room down the hall, along with some extra clothes that we keep on hand for emergencies."

"Thanks, Darrin. I know this is inconvenient having us—"

"Nola, you're family. You know that. And those three look as if they could use a little help. You never have to apologize for coming here with or without a few strays in tow."

Nola nodded, grateful for his help.

A yawn cut across Darrin's face. Nola had to swallow her own in response.

Darrin chuckled. "Gone are the days when I could stay up till three in the morning. Now I'm yawning when it's eight thirty." He glanced at the clock. "Ten o'clock is an hour I haven't seen in a long time. Why don't you take my room? I'll sleep on the couch."

Nola shook her head. "No. I'll take the couch."

Darrin studied her. "Because you need to be the first line of defense if somebody comes through the door."

She shrugged. "I like couches."

Darrin chuckled. "Sure. Well, this old man isn't going to fight you. My bones have definitely grown accustomed to a bed. Do you need anything?"

Nola shook her head. She'd grabbed her bag on the way in, which had all her overnight essentials. Not that she was planning on throwing on some PJs. "I'm good."

"Then I wish you pleasant dreams. And it's good to see you, Nola."

Darrin hugged her. Nola found her arms wrapping around him as well. "You too."

Darrin gave her one last smile before heading down the hall and closing the door to his bedroom.

Nola headed down the hall as well, quickly stopping in the bathroom to wash up, change her clothes, and brush her teeth. She was back out of the bathroom in less than five minutes. She turned to the right instead of heading to the living room and peeked into the room that the Ortiz family had been given.

Rafe sat up in bed with the kids curled up on either side, his arms wrapped protectively around them. But Rafe's eyes were closed. It was a good sign that he was able to sleep. Sleep meant he felt secure, at least for the moment. And he was going to need that sleep. He needed to be on his game. The better rested he was, the better he'd be able to do that.

And the deeper he slept, the easier her next task would be. She quickly grabbed what she needed, went back into the living room, and booted up her laptop. Five minutes later, she was done. After one more trip into the room with the Ortizes, she made her way back to the living room, feeling the effects of today and yesterday. She arched her back as she walked, trying to loosen some of the tightness. But it wasn't stretches she needed. She hadn't gotten much sleep this morning, and she desperately needed some now.

She sat down on the couch, slipping her gun under the pillow that Darrin had placed there. She kicked off her boots and pulled the blanket over her as she lay down. Just a little sleep, and then she'd see what needed to be done.

THE ROOM WAS STILL DARK when Nola's eyes flew open. She reached slowly underneath her pillow for the gun, making sure to stay still to not allow whoever had stepped into the room to know she was awake. She scanned the room, keeping her breathing even.

A nightlight plugged into an outlet over by the hallway showed a small figure slipping into the room.

Nola relaxed her hold on her gun. Enzo crept closer to the couch and then stood directly in front of her.

Nola remembered when Molly used to do the same thing. It would scare the heck out of David, who wouldn't realize Molly was there until she was right next to the bed, looking like some sort of murderer in the dark. But Nola had always heard her as soon as her feet hit the floor. And then she would simply open up her blankets and Molly would crawl in. The two would snuggle before falling back to sleep.

But Enzo was not Molly. And Nola wasn't sure what she was supposed to do here. She sat up slowly. "Is everything all right, Enzo?"

He shook his head.

There was no noise coming from down the hall, so she knew that nothing had happened to his father or his sister. She studied the little boy who'd been traumatized since his mother's death. That trauma had no doubt been compounded by what had happened today.

"Are you scared?" she asked softly.

He nodded, clutching his puppy in his arms tighter.

"I don't blame you. Today was scary."

Enzo's gaze darted to the bear in the corner. Nola followed his gaze. "Are you scared of the bear?"

Enzo nodded again.

Nola let out a breath. Now this, she could handle. "Oh, there's no need to be scared of Smokey."

She patted the couch next to her. After a moment's hesitation, Enzo hopped up on it and sat looking up at her with his big eyes.

"Smokey there is the protector of the camp. You see, she's a guardian. And although she looks scary, there's a reason for that: She protects everybody who lives at this camp and all the guests that come here, which includes you. So you never have to worry about Smokey hurting you. But if anybody were to try and hurt you, well, then Smokey would come to life in a second and protect you."

Enzo stared at the bear and then looked back at Nola. "Like you'll protect us?"

Nola stared down at him, knowing he was looking for a promise. And even though she knew she shouldn't make promises she couldn't keep, she found herself nodding. "Like I'll protect you."

Enzo gave his own nod and then curled up on the side of the couch. Nola hesitated for a moment, thinking she should probably take the boy back to his room. But he looked so peaceful curled up there. She took the blanket and wrapped it around him, promising herself that she'd carry him back to his father in just a few minutes, after he'd fallen asleep.

CHAPTER TWENTY-ONE

RAFE

LIGHT WAS BARELY COMING in the through the blinds when Rafe jolted awake. His heart pounded and his mouth felt dry as he stared wildly around the room. The nightmare hung on even as he acknowledged that it wasn't real.

The cartel had come for him and his family. And this time he had missed when he reached out to grab Sofia and Enzo. The two of them had died in front of his eyes before bursting into flames.

He ran his hands over his face, trying to wipe away the images. But they stubbornly stayed at the front of his mind.

Next to him, Sofia murmured softly in her sleep and then rolled over. He tucked the blanket back around her. He reached over to tuck in Enzo.

He wasn't there.

Rafe looked on the floor to see if maybe he'd fallen, but the space was empty.

His heart began to pound wildly even as he slipped quietly out of the bed, not wanting to disturb Sofia. He hustled down the hall and stopped at the bathroom, but it was dark. Darrin's bedroom door was closed. He passed it and headed toward the living room.

He stopped short.

Enzo was curled up asleep on the couch. Nola lay behind him, her arm protectively wrapped around him.

Rafe took a step back, needing to hold on to the wall for a moment. Enzo had barely interacted with anyone since his mother had died. The whole trip to the United States, he'd kept his eyes down, making no eye contact and shying away from anyone's touch. At school, he'd struggled to fit in.

But now he lay perfectly content, curled up with a woman they had met only a few hours ago.

Rafe didn't know what to make of that. It was progress, of that he was absolutely sure. And in his former life, he would've said that he placed his trust in children's judgment of people over almost anyone else's.

But now he was all too aware of how easily it was to get fooled.

At the same time, he couldn't help but hope that maybe, just maybe, this was the beginning of Enzo coming back to them.

He studied the unusual woman who held his son protectively in her arms. She was beautiful. She was tough. And Darrin was right, she was like a gunslinger of old doing what was right no matter the cost.

He prayed that that cost wasn't her life and that Enzo wasn't forced to deal with another loss of someone he'd reached out to.

And at the same time, he prayed that his son's faith in her was not misplaced.

CHAPTER TWENTY-TWO

NOLA

NOLA WOKE UP SLOWLY, a rarity in her world. She felt warm, comfortably warm. With a jolt, she realized a small body was curled up next to her. She must've fallen asleep after Enzo had come in, and then at some point, he'd switched sides of the couch to sleep next to her.

Shock raced through her at the feel of his little body curled up next to her. The memory of Molly doing the same thing years ago surged into her mind. For just a moment, she let herself pretend it was Molly asleep next to her.

But Nola wasn't one to live in fantasies for long. She gently placed a hand on his side. His chest moved in and out. He was still lost in sleep. Her eyes flew to the wall across the room as Rafe pushed himself off the wall and walked toward her.

She felt unsettled that she hadn't heard him come in. She

kept her voice down as she spoke. "He came in last night. I was going to bring him back after he curled up on the couch, but I must've fallen asleep. I didn't mean to—"

Rafe shook his head as he ran a hand over his son's hair. "It's all right. I'm just glad that he trusted you enough to come to you."

Darrin stepped out of the hallway. His eyes grew large as he took in the scene, and then with a smile he headed to the kitchen.

Rafe gently wrapped his arms underneath Enzo and picked him up. Enzo curled into his father's chest without waking. Rafe carried him back down the hall.

Nola immediately felt a little colder once Enzo's small body was removed. She took a couple of deep breaths, trying to hold back the tide. She wasn't sure what emotions were rushing over her: sadness, a longing for a time that would never be, warmth, and maybe happiness?

She sat up slowly, feeling strange.

While Darrin was busy getting breakfast together, Nola put a hand to her mouth and then grabbed her gun from underneath the pillow. Snatching her jacket from the coffee table, she strode outside. The cold slapped against her skin the moment she stepped out the door. Slipping on her jacket, she stepped to the edge of the porch and closed her eyes, grateful for the chill in the air.

And the reality check it brought. She had a job to do.

The cabins with the kids had begun to stir. Teachers and counselors walked amongst them, waking people up and getting them ready for the day. Nola held on to the porch railing, watching the early morning routine.

She walked down the stairs and headed toward the security hut. She wanted to make sure there'd been no problems last night. But even though the security hut was far from the main house, she still felt as if a string was connecting her to the people back there, especially the little boy.

And for the first time in a long time, in the dark recesses of her mind, she could admit that she welcomed the connection.

CHAPTER TWENTY-THREE

BISHOP

BISHOP WALKED into the old brick warehouse, glancing around her. Today she was technically working for the CIA. But she wasn't in the mood to deal with Langley, so she'd decided to work in her own dedicated office space.

She'd called into the office on the drive over and told them that she'd be working from home today. They knew what her setup was and had no problem with it.

Truth was, if she said she was going to full-time work from home, they would have had no problem with that either. But she liked going into an office some days and interacting with other people. Otherwise it was just her and the computers. And while they allowed her access to a world of information, they were no substitute for human contact.

She'd created this setup with David and Nola's help years ago. It now housed her computers and had a loft upstairs, where she slept. Technically, it was her apartment, she supposed. But it wasn't her home. Her home was Ileana's estate. She'd moved there after she'd left Nola and David's home. She'd wanted to be more independent, but she hadn't been ready for her own place. Ileana was a good compromise. She'd stayed there most weekends and at the loft during the week.

Then David and Molly had died. Everything had changed. She'd gone from staying at Ileana's on weekends to full-time. With Nola gone, Bishop needed to be around people who cared about her. Now she rarely stayed at her loft. But on the days when she didn't have time to make the trek out to the estate, this was where she laid her head.

Today she had the time to go out to the estate, but she wanted to check a few more things on Nola's latest case.

She let herself in, sliding the heavy door back and then locking it behind her. She flipped on the lights. Outside, no one would know that the lights were on. She had installed a special glass so that it always appeared as if the warehouse was unoccupied.

The warehouse was old, dating back to the 1950s. It had formerly been a shoe factory. The remnants of the old conveyor belts were still strewn up above. Bishop liked looking at them. They made her feel as if she was part of the history of the place. In her mind's eye, she could see the workers scurrying around, taking shoes off the conveyor belt, inspecting them, and placing them in boxes. It had been a simpler time in a lot of ways.

Well, simpler for white people at least. And men. Someone like her, half black, half Middle Eastern, and female to boot, would not have fared so well.

But she ignored the cultural shifts in her imaginings. In her mind, the melting pot of people that were employed at the shoe factory were going on about their work like busy little bees. Or

Smurfs, which was how she actually thought of it: a grown-up Smurf village.

Bishop slipped her messenger bag off her shoulder and onto her desk. Desk was a misnomer. It was a half circle that was ten feet long. Six screens covered the wall in front of her, and she had multiple servers lined up on either side. All of the servers and the computing equipment were locked behind a mesh structure. She opened the door and let herself in the faraday cage. She didn't want anyone to know that there was activity coming from here, and she certainly wasn't going to take the chance of someone hacking in. Faraday cages weren't a guarantee, but they definitely made it more difficult.

She walked over to the Keurig and quickly made herself a cup of coffee. After taking a sip, she let out a sigh. When she was younger, she'd hated coffee. She loved the smell of it, but the taste of it was something she just couldn't get used to. Working for the CIA for the last few years, she'd grown accustomed to the taste, and now, like most every other adult on the planet, she craved it.

She slipped the top onto her reusable coffee mug and took a seat, then tapped a few keys on the keyboard. She sat, her eyes scanning the screens as the programs that had been working all night provided their summaries. Most were related to cases she was working on for the CIA. Sometimes she liked to use her own equipment out of the confines of the office. Plus, her computers were faster. The government was many things, but on top of their tech was not one of them.

And, of course, she couldn't run the information she needed for Nola's cases on CIA computers. Right now, she was running the background on Rafael Ortiz along with half a dozen searches for the CIA.

An ongoing case search for the CIA had found a few hits. She scribbled off a quick note to the appropriate Langley contact and sent him the relevant findings.

Then she turned her attention to the background on Rafe. On screen were images from the remnants of the Ortizes' home back in Mexico. There was nothing left. It had been burnt down to the studs. It was a miracle any of them had survived.

She quickly shifted from that to the intake interview at Immigration. According to the agent, the father had demonstrated credible fear. He'd been quickly linked up with a US district attorney.

The district attorney had then hooked him up with a handler to oversee his case and to give him an identity that would keep them hidden for a little while until he could be put into the witness protection program.

Bishop pulled up the picture they had of Rafael Ortiz. He was a handsome man. Check that, he was hot. Dark smoldering eyes, black hair, strong build. Definitely a bit of eye candy.

The kids were cute. The son looked like the father, but the daughter took after the mother.

Bishop focused on the daughter and the son. They were eight and six.

The daughter had long dark hair just like Molly had. When Bishop had first seen the photo of the family, she wondered if Nola had noticed.

Then she'd rolled her eyes at the idea that Nola hadn't. There was very little that escaped Nola's attention. Of course she'd noticed that Sofia's hair was like her daughter's. And it was having a strong impact on her. For Nola to mention it last night, it had to. She hadn't said anything like that in . . . Actually, Bishop couldn't remember her ever saying something like that. It had been unusual.

But Bishop wondered what kind of impact that would have on her.

Ever since the case down in Georgia, Nola had been different. She'd been slowly coming back to the land of the living. She wasn't back to the way she had been before, but she'd been at Ileana's estate on two other occasions since then. Being that in the past two years, she'd been there exactly zero times, Bishop thought it was a good sign.

Bishop flipped screens to see what was happening with the people from the Georgia case. Nola had asked her to keep an eye on them, another break from her pattern. Normally, when Nola was finished with a case, she was finished. But something about Georgia had been different.

Rascal Nealon was now the chief of police. Bishop had quietly gathered as much material as she could on the corruption in the Delford PD and then sent all of it anonymously to the district attorney. There'd been a full-scale investigation, followed by more than a few police officers losing their badges, and a few more ending up in prison. Rascal was now in charge, and by all accounts, seemed to be doing a good job.

Ileana had created a rehab center from one of the old mansions that was falling to ruin on the edge of Delford. She'd had it renovated and turned into a home for the girls who'd been caught up in the human trafficking situation. Twelve girls now lived at the home. There were also counseling services on site that both Anna Mae and Natalie had taken advantage of. Charlene was also taking advantage of the rehab and had re-enrolled in school.

Teddy Haverford and Anna Mae still looked like they were going strong as the best of buds. All in all, things in Georgia had turned out better than anyone had expected.

Especially Bishop.

Now Bishop stared at the remaining members of the Ortiz family, wondering if their outcome would be as good. They had been through a lot. Just like Nola had. She was hoping that Nola would be able to help them. After all, it was what she did. But she wondered if maybe the Ortiz family could help her out just as much.

Bishop continued to scroll through her feed in the warehouse, munching on a breakfast sandwich that she'd picked up after she'd woken up this morning.

Her coffee had a hint of hazelnut. It had been a good choice.

She scanned the files, looking to see if anything new had popped up on Nola's case. But so far it looked like everything was at a standstill. A light in the corner of the monitor second from the right blinked. She clicked on it and smiled.

Apparently the coroner had finally submitted the autopsy results on the two cops from Massapequa. Normally an autopsy would take a few days minimum, but she wasn't surprised that when it was cops, the autopsy moved much quicker. She scanned the file, checking for the cause of death. First victim: gunshot wound. No surprise there.

The other victim had been killed by suffocation brought on by a broken neck. Again, not exactly a surprise.

However, there was an addendum attached to the files. That was unusual.

She flipped over to it and started to read while taking another bite of her sandwich. She stopped mid-chew, staring at the screen. She swallowed quickly and started to cough as she nearly choked on her food. She grabbed her coffee and downed it, coughing a few more times while she reached for her phone.

CHAPTER TWENTY-FOUR

NOLA

"THEY WEREN'T COPS."

Those were the first words out of Bishop's mouth as Nola answered her call. She'd been heading back to the main cabin when her phone rang. "What?"

"The two guys in Rafe's apartment. They weren't police officers."

Nola stopped, her eyes narrowing. "Then who were they?" she asked, although she had a sneaking suspicion she knew.

"Both of them have lengthy arrest records. It looks like they were guns for hire. I'm betting they boosted the cop car from a garage that services them. I'm not sure yet where they got the uniforms. The older guy and younger guy apparently linked up while doing time. They both had just gotten out within the last three months."

"Who sent them?"

Nola could hear Bishop's frustration across the line. "I don't know yet. Tracking it down as we speak. This is good news, though, right?"

This was definitely good news. With the results, hopefully the police would no longer be gunning for Rafe in the same way. Which hopefully meant that was one less bull's-eye on his back.

Of course, the rest of the bull's-eyes remained, but that was a separate issue.

"I'm sending the files over to some media contacts and the district attorney that's reviewing his former handler's old cases. This should hopefully push Rafe's case to the top of the pile."

"Good, that's good."

"You guys safe?"

"We're good. Keep an ear out, will you?"

"Always."

"Great. Thanks, Bishop."

Nola could hear the smile in Bishop's voice. "Anytime."

Nola pocketed her phone, a smile upon her lips. She missed Bishop. She'd missed all of this.

But once again, she shoved the feelings of warmth aside. It wasn't the time for it. Right now, the Ortiz family needed her complete and total focus. Because while hopefully this meant that the cops were off their tail, it wasn't going to help with MS-13. She was on the far side of the camp. She'd wanted to walk the perimeter again, but she'd seen no red flags. Deciding to head back, she picked up her pace. A talk with Rafe was in order.

By the time Nola made it back to the main house, both kids were up and sitting at the table eating pancakes. Sean, Darrin's unofficial boyfriend and the camp cook, had arrived. He smiled when Nola stepped in the door. "Aren't you a sight for sore eyes?"

Small and slim, Sean had a pale complexion thanks to his Irish ancestors and the red hair to boot. In appearance, they were complete opposites. Darrin tended more to a hippy vibe while

Sean was almost always in dockers and polo shirts. Yet somehow when you saw them together, they just made sense.

"Morning, Sean. Good to see you too."

Sean smiled back at her. "I got pancakes. You want some?"

"Maybe in a little bit." She turned to Rafe, who was sitting in front of a cleared plate, sipping coffee. "I need to speak with you."

Rafe looked at the kids.

"I've got them. Go on." Sean waved him away as he bustled out of the kitchen with a plate of cinnamon buns and placed them in front of Sofia and Enzo. The two kids' faces lit up at the sight of them.

Rafe rolled his eyes. "All right, you two, you can have a cinnamon bun. But you are *definitely* having some vegetables later."

"Okay, Dad," Sofia said as she reached for one of the sticky buns.

Still shaking his head, Rafe stood up, kissing each of the kids on the forehead before crossing the room to Nola. She nodded toward the door. "We can talk out on the porch."

A furrow appeared between Rafe's brows, but he didn't say anything as he followed her outside. She led him to the far side of the porch on the opposite side of the house from the kitchen and leaned against the porch railing, her arms crossed over her chest. "The two men in your apartment weren't cops. They were guns for hire."

Rafe's steps faltered before he continued. He leaned his hip against the railing. "What?"

Nola gave him the rundown on the details that Bishop had provided about the two assailants. Rafe's face shifted from shock to anger. "The cartel."

Nola gave him an abrupt nod. "That's what I figure as well."

"So the police know that I'm not a cop killer?"

"I have a friend making sure that the details are spread far and wide. She even sent the info to the media."

Rafe's shoulders sagged. He ran a hand through his hair. "I thought I killed two cops."

Nola gave him a moment, knowing he needed to work through the emotions. "But you didn't. What you did was protect yourself and your family."

Rafe took a deep breath, ran his hands over his face, and then straightened. "Okay, so what does this mean?"

"Well, hopefully it means that the State Department and the DOJ will now be pushing you to the head of the line. No guarantee on that front, of course, but it seems the most likely scenario. I have another friend that's going to be using her influence to try and make sure that that happens."

Rafe let out a breath. "You have some good friends."

"I guess I do. But it doesn't solve the problem of MS-13 being after us. Why do they think that you killed one of their members?"

Rafe shifted so he was practically sitting on the railing. "I don't know. It must have to do with that kid that was killed at the school not that long ago. He was somehow linked to an MS-13 member, a nephew of one of the members, I think. He was killed behind the soccer fields of the high school where I work. It was a brutal killing. It had all the hallmarks of a gang killing. The cops were all over the place for a few days, asking kids, getting surveillance tapes, the whole nine yards. They never found anything. Most assumed it was the 18th Street because of the rivalry. There was another boy killed a few months back. He was an 18th Street member. The rumor was that the killing at the soccer field was payback."

"How are you tied into it?"

"That's the thing—I'm not. I mean, I vaguely recall seeing the kid at school, but I never interacted with him. My days are getting the kids to school, getting myself to the high school, and then heading home and being with the kids."

"Do you ever go out at night?"

Rafe shook his head. "No. Never. Not the entire time we've been here. Besides school, they haven't left my side since . . ."

"Since Mexico."

He nodded. "They're still going through a lot of trauma, and I just couldn't do it."

"Can anyone testify to that?"

"No one besides Sofia and Enzo. I mean, if anybody said that they saw me outside the apartment, they'd be lying."

Nola nodded.

Rafe's voice was heavy when he spoke. "If the cartel found out where I was, I wouldn't be surprised if they spread the rumor. They want me dead. They don't really care how it happens. And it would be just like them to have a backup plan if the hitmen didn't work."

"I was thinking the same thing. But it doesn't change the problem that MS-13 is still looking for you."

Rafe nodded, looking out over the camp. He didn't speak for a few moments, and Nola didn't either. She was trying to figure out where they would go next. They couldn't stay at Darrin's more than another night. It wouldn't be safe for any of them, including Darrin's kids.

But she didn't like any of their options yet for where to go.

The truth was, until they had this settled, there would be no safe ground. Until they were in government protection, they would have to keep moving. It would be the only way to ensure that they were safe.

And that wasn't a perfect guarantee anyway. They'd have to find someplace untouched by any sort of surveillance and completely free of gang activity. And at the same time, they'd have to make sure that they didn't leave a trail getting there. She didn't like their odds, especially if they were taking Enzo and Sofia with them.

Rafe turned away from the camp and looked into Nola's eyes. "The gangs want me. If it comes down to it, I need you to do something for me."

Nola knew what he was going to say before he even said it.

"If it comes to a choice and there's no out, you take the kids and run. Leave me behind. Just get them somewhere safe, somewhere they can be taken care of. Somewhere that someone will look after them and hopefully, one day, love them."

Nola looked into his eyes and read the commitment there as well as the pain. And she knew it well. Because if she'd had the choice, she would've sacrificed herself willingly so that Molly could live. So instead of arguing with him or giving him false hope, she simply nodded.

"I will."

CHAPTER TWENTY-FIVE

RAFE

EVEN THOUGH RAFE and the kids were confined within the walls of Darrin's camp, it almost felt like a vacation. Or at least, as close to one as they'd had in the last two years. Darrin had given them fishing rods, and they'd fished off the dock at the lake. And despite the cold, they'd picnicked next to the lake for lunch. And when they'd gone back to the main house, they'd made s'mores.

Now the kids were playing at the playground they'd seen the night before. The looks of joy on their faces were pretty amazing. Rafe knew that this was just a small little break from the horror that was currently their lives. A mirage that would soon fade away.

But he tried to keep that fatalism from his expression. The kids were happy right now, and the fact that they felt safe after everything they'd been through, well, that was worth more than he could say.

He glanced over to where Nola stood leaning against a tree, occasionally watching the kids but more often watching their surroundings. She had stayed with the family the whole day. And she was a big part of the reason that the kids felt safe, especially Enzo. Every once in a while, Rafe would catch him glancing over to see if Nola was still there. And when he realized she was, he would go right back to playing.

Nola made Enzo feel safe. And Rafe understood that. There was something about her that just said that she could handle whatever was thrown her way.

At the same time, he could see the pain that she was hiding. It was like a coat that she wore each day without even thinking about. He wondered what that story was and if that was why she was so focused now on keeping his family safe. She had to have lost someone—he just wondered who exactly they had been to her. Whoever it was, they had obviously been important to her.

"Daddy, push me!" Sofia went over to the swings and hopped on.

He blew out a breath as he moved toward her. "Push you? I think I've pushed you enough today. This has to be like the twelfth time."

"Please, Papa!"

Rafe faked an exasperated sigh. "Okay, fine."

He stepped behind her and then tickled her at the waist. She giggled, squirming in her seat. He pushed the swing, smiling at Sofia's joy. It was contagious.

Enzo sat in the sandbox, filling a bucket with sand. Nola had gone and gotten them the bucket and then some water to make the sand a little more packable. Enzo had now created a small fortress around him that he sat in the middle of.

All in all, right now was a much better situation than he could have even possibly imagined twenty-four hours earlier. He'd been desperate, scrambling to figure out some way to protect his family. And then Nola had arrived and extended a rope. She pulled them out and gave them hope. No matter what happened from this moment on, he would be forever grateful for that.

CHAPTER TWENTY-SIX

NOLA

NOLA WATCHED the little family as they played. Each time Sofia let out a giggle, it was like a dagger to her chest. The laugh was so much like Molly's. And her hair . . . When she was on the swing, it covered her face when she swung back. It was hard not to think that it was Molly, carefree and laughing, just a few dozen feet away from her.

Sofia was difficult to watch, so Nola kept her attention on Enzo. He'd created a circle of sand structures, then he placed himself inside. He'd created a wall of protection for himself.

Nola completely understood the inclination. She'd done the same to herself for the last two years. Even though she knew that for her it was the right call, she didn't want that for Enzo. He was too young to live his life alone.

She shook herself from her thoughts. Once again, the job was getting to her. Six months ago in Georgia, the job had gotten to her. She'd taken over a dozen jobs in between, but none of them had touched her the same way Anna Mae's case had down in Georgia.

She even had Bishop keeping tabs on them to make sure that everyone was doing all right. And so far it looked like they were. Rascal had even reached out and left Nola a few voicemails, just explaining about what was going on and what he was up to. Nola had shocked herself by returning one of those calls. She did it at night when she knew he'd be sleeping, but she left a message congratulating him on his new role and wishing him luck. And she'd meant it. Rascal was a good man, a good cop. And the people of Delford deserved someone like him.

She wasn't sure that such an ending was in store for the Ortiz family, however. Even with the cops no longer viewing him as a cop killer, he'd still killed two men in his apartment. And it was not beyond the pale to see someone thinking that Rafe hadn't known they weren't cops. Therefore, in their minds, he could still be a cop killer.

Plus, he was an immigrant who killed two men in his apartment. In the current political climate, there wasn't a lot of compassion for that. It didn't matter that it had been in self-defense. For some people, he would just be a killer.

And then, of course, there was the fact that both the cartel and MS-13 were still after him. She needed to get him off the island. And she needed to do it in a way that ensured no one knew where they were going. If Bishop didn't call today or tomorrow morning at the latest, Nola would have to figure it out on her own. In her mind, she'd already plotted out a route that would take them along the northern portion of the United States.

But she really hoped it didn't come to that. She didn't want the kids having to spend the next couple months on the run. Not after all they'd been through. They needed to set down some roots. They needed normalcy.

She knew that they were traumatized by what had happened at the motel yesterday, but they were currently in denial. They'd shoved all those thoughts and memories to the far recesses of their minds. But one day, they would come to the forefront, and they would need help getting through them. And being on the run wouldn't be any good for that.

She shifted position against the tree and crossed her feet at the ankles. They were in a quiet part of the camp, although every once in a while she could hear some kids talking or laughing from just beyond the trees. Darrin had done a really amazing thing here. He himself had a pretty dark and violent gang history. But he'd found Jesus about thirty years ago and changed his ways. He'd been in deep out on the West Coast but had decided to move out east for a fresh start. And it had worked well for him and for all the kids that he'd helped. Part of Nola wondered if maybe she should leave Sofia and Enzo with him and just take Rafe on the run. It would be easier. It would be safer for the kids. But she knew Rafe would never agree to it. Not yet, anyway.

And if she had been in his shoes, she wouldn't have either.

So it looked like they were all going to be getting into the car and heading out tomorrow. She'd have to call Avad and arrange for different transportation. The Bronco was a great car, but it wasn't meant for long trips for a group, nor was it meant for speed.

Plus she needed to stock up on ammo. She was running low. She'd planned on heading back to Ileana's estate after the Jersey job and restocking. But then she'd gotten the call about Rafael and his family, so she hadn't had the time. She was down to four magazines, and that was it.

If push came to shove, she could always stop at a gun shop and load up. But gun shops weren't exactly located in the best parts of most towns. And she didn't really want to take the Ortiz family there. She also didn't want to leave them behind while she went off running errands. She was in a serious damned if you, do damned if you don't situation.

Her phone rang, and she glanced down at it before she answered it. "Ileana."

The warmth in Ileana's voice flowed out of the phone. "Nola. It is good to hear your voice. How are the Ortizes?"

"As good as can be expected. They're a good family, a strong one. They care about one another. It'll get them through this."

"That was my read on them as well. And I have some good news on that front. A meeting has been arranged with Rafael's new handler. There still are, of course, some questions about the situation out in Massapequa, but if all goes well at the interview, he and his family will immediately be put into the witness protection program."

Nola let out a breath, although her gaze strayed to Enzo. She felt a small pinch of loss at the idea of not seeing him again. But this was what was best for him and his family.

"That's great. When and where?"

"Tomorrow morning, nine a.m. The meeting will be at a safehouse in Flushing."

Nola frowned. Flushing was a densely populated area. She did not like the idea of bringing the family in there. There were too many variables that she couldn't control. "I don't like that."

Ileana sighed. "I knew you wouldn't. I don't like it either. But the new handler was insistent. His office is in Manhattan, and I get the feeling he didn't want to travel too far."

Nola rolled her eyes. "Great, a bureaucrat. He's probably never been in the field and has no idea what his clients have been through. What do you know about the handler?"

"I'm afraid you're right about him. He's a new US DA. He was a Supreme Court clerk until six months ago."

"Field experience?"

"Nothing outside of a video game console," Ileana said dryly.

Nola groaned. "You can't be serious."

"I'm afraid I am. But hopefully this will only be a short-term arrangement. I'm pushing them to assign a more seasoned individual."

Nola shook her head. A meeting in people-packed Flushing she did not like. A newbie handler in charge of it she liked even less. "How long will it take to get someone more experienced?"

"Too long. There's no guarantee I can even make it happen. I'm afraid this is as good as it gets right now."

Nola gritted her teeth. *Damn it.* "Is the guy trustworthy?"

Ileana hesitated. "I don't know. There are no red flags in his file, and Bishop's doing a deep search, but I'm afraid this one's going to have to be a matter of trust."

Nola nodded, realizing the truth in her statement and knowing that trust was not something that she gave easily. And she didn't intend to give it easily at this point either.

"I'm going to need some more supplies."

"I figured as much. I set up a meeting for you for tomorrow, early. Avad will be there to load you up and back you up."

Nola shook her head. "I'd prefer if we could do it tonight."

"I thought you might. I'll get back to you with the details if I can arrange it."

"Okay. Thanks."

"And Nola?"

"Yeah?"

"Take care of that family."

Nola's gaze shifted from each member of the Ortiz family. "I will."

CHAPTER TWENTY-SEVEN

BISHOP

THE YAWN THREATENED to swallow Bishop whole. She rubbed her eyes, staring at the monitors. She'd spent the day working through a gunrunning case. It turned out to be a little bit more complicated than planned. But finally she got all the information and enough evidence for a search warrant of the company's US holdings in Portland. And with that information, she'd made both the CIA and the FBI happy, a decidedly rare accomplishment.

That meant she could finally get back to work on Nola's case. She stood up and stretched her back, stepping out of the cage and walking over to the kitchen underneath her loft. The fridge had few options, which wasn't surprising.

She grabbed the pizza box from last night and placed it on the counter. After turning on the toaster oven, she grabbed two slices and put them on the tray before sliding them in. She grabbed some water and refilled her water container.

She needed to cut down on the caffeine or she was never going to sleep tonight. But at the same time, she could really use a jolt. She took a sip of the water and then pushed the water aside. *That's not going to cut it.*

She went back to the fridge and pulled out a Diet Pepsi. Pulling a glass from the cabinet, she poured the soda in, adding some ice. She took a sip and let out a sigh. *That's better.*

After another few minutes, she grabbed the pizza from the toaster oven. It wasn't extremely warm, but it would have to do. She hated microwaving pizza. Something about it just seemed wrong.

Balancing her plate on her arm, she walked back to the cage and opened the door with one hand. She placed her food and drink back on the desk before turning and closing the door. After sitting down in her seat, she realized she'd forgotten napkins.

She groaned, looking back across the warehouse. Too far. A quick search through her desk came up with two unused napkins in the back of her top drawer. She placed them on the counter and then grabbed a slice of pizza and took a bite. The mix of cheese, spices, and tomato sauce swirled around in her mouth, and she sighed.

She could live on pizza. If she were stranded on a desert island and only had one food that she was allowed to bring, without a doubt, she would choose pizza.

With a sip of her drink, she hit a few buttons on her keyboard. Searches related to Nola's case flashed across the screens. Taking a few more bites, she contentedly watched the information, seeing what was going on.

The news had released information that the two "police officers" were not that at all. It appeared that they had also stolen the squad car from a garage that did repairs for the police department, as Bishop had suspected. The uniforms had come from the police station. Apparently they had an inside man.

Chiefs of both the Massapequa and Hempstead Police Departments had made a joint statement saying that they would be working together to run down how this was possible and to make sure that safeguards were put in place so that it never happened again.

Bishop rolled her eyes at that. That was some serious CYA. Criminals always found ways to get around any sort of defenses that were put in place.

Heck, it was Bishop's job to get around any sort of computer safeguards that people put into place. That was just the nature of the beast. It was a constant game of one-upmanship, with everybody always trying to up their game that then resulted in their opponent also upping their game. But she supposed that was what the public wanted to hear. It made them feel safe, even though it shouldn't.

The chiefs also said that they were still interested in speaking with Ralph Smith to learn what exactly had happened. They did, however, focus on the criminal records of both of the men who had been killed. The narrative had shifted from making him sound like the FBI's most wanted to a slightly less wanted, more like Massapequa's top five. Which was definitely better. But it meant that if anybody caught sight of Rafe, the police would immediately be notified.

Not ideal.

Bishop was still trying to figure out how MS-13 had been led to believe that Rafe was behind the murder in Islip. That just made no sense.

She was sure that the cartel was behind it, although how they'd gotten word to MS-13 was still beyond her.

And that annoyed her.

There weren't a lot of cases where she couldn't track down the information she wanted. This case, though, was proving to be elusive. She knew that the cartel had to be communicating electronically. They certainly weren't going to swing by and have a heart-to-heart with some random gang members in Massapequa, New York. She'd tracked down a few suspected cartel members in the New York area and was tracking their phones, but so far, she hadn't found any mention of Rafe's family or any calls to MS-13 members.

She pushed aside her food, and after wiping her hands, quickly brought up the algorithm she'd been working for that particular problem. An expanded connection search was in order for all the cell phones of any alleged gang member. That way she could cross tabs with any unknown numbers. That was going to be a huge job, but it was the only path forward. Then she would cross-reference that with all of the known cartel members and any unknown numbers that they were dialing. If she was lucky, she'd find a connection.

A beep sounded. Bishop looked up, scanning the monitors to see which alarm had gone off when she realized it was her cell phone. She picked it up. It was a text from Ileana. She'd just spoken with the US District Attorney's office and told Nola what the meeting place was going to be tomorrow.

Bishop placed the phone back on the counter, turning her attention back to the search for a link between the Long Island gang and the cartel. But her mind drifted over what Ileana had said. She really did still have a lot of sway, even though she'd been out of the intelligence world for a few years.

Bishop watched the numbers scroll by on her screen. Links began to appear. They sure did call a lot of untraceable phones. That was not surprising.

Bishop stopped still, shifting toward her own cell phone. Ileana said the handler was relatively new. That could mean nothing. Most came from other agencies, so "new" didn't necessarily mean inexperienced. But still . . .

She ran a quick search on the new handler: Christian Anderson, age twenty-nine. Even she winced at the age. She ran a quick background check and realized her wince was well-deserved. Anderson had zero field experience. He'd only had three other cases, all low level.

A trickling of concern had shifted to a steady flow.

Bishop ran the guy's background. Nothing stood out, no legal or financial issues. He seemed to live within his means. But that wasn't where the danger could come from.

Taking a breath, she paused, her hands above the keyboard. What she was about to do was decidedly illegal. Occasionally she did so at the behest of the CIA and Nola. But she'd never had to break into a US attorney's files. Maybe she should call Ileana.

But she discarded the thought almost as soon as she had it. It would take Ileana too long to get the information she needed, if she even managed it.

Well, here goes nothing. It took her five minutes to break into Anderson's files. It should have taken her longer. The guy had practically zero security on his personal computer, and he stupidly had a ton of work files on there. There was even a file on Rafe. Bishop quickly scanned the information available on the attack at the Sayonara Motel. It had only been a small newspaper article. Apparently even that kind a gang fight didn't warrant a lot of attention.

Video had been uploaded online. It was from after the violence had died down. Anderson had added that to his file as well. It was just a quick shot of Nola moving the family to her car to get out. Bishop stopped the frame. There was a close-up of Nola. It was blurry, but there were programs that could clean up an image and give them a sharper view.

Which meant the cartel would know that Nola was helping out the Ortizes. *Damn it.*

Anderson had also included Nola's government file, the one with all her connections, including Darrin.

But that wasn't the worst of it. The guy kept a daily planner online.

He listed the meeting with Rafael by name, and the location. Bishop stared at it, dumbstruck. How stupid was this guy?

And if she could get the information this easily, anybody else could. The government at times leaked like a sieve. And the cartel was very good at exploiting those leaks.

She grabbed her phone and dialed quickly.

CHAPTER TWENTY-EIGHT

NOLA

TEN MINUTES AGO, the camp's residents had all filed into the large cabin used as a cafeteria. The grounds were quiet now. The cafeteria also had a living room area where they were showing a movie later tonight. Rafe had taken his kids into the main house to get washed up for dinner. Nola stood out on the porch, looking around. Everything was quiet. Everything was calm.

Yet she was completely unsettled.

She felt like there was a tidal wave rushing toward them that they couldn't yet see. The police had calmed down their search for Rafe but hadn't completely stopped looking for him. MS-13 and the cartel were still fervently focused on him.

Yet she was just standing here, waiting.

She walked to the edge of the porch. Grabbing the railing, she scanned the camp. Maybe she should take that trip to the gun store and just pick up some supplies. Having a few extra maga-zines always made a girl feel a little more secure.

The sound of Sofia's voice came softly through the window. It was muffled, so she couldn't make out the words, but there was no alarm or concern in her tone.

Nola walked over to the window and glanced inside. Sofia was helping Darrin carry dinner out to the table. Rafe was behind the counter, placing food on plates while Enzo set out silverware at different settings on the table. It was a very familial scene. Enzo looked up as if feeling Nola's eyes on him. He met her gaze for a long moment and then bent back to his task.

Nola couldn't leave them here without her. It would most likely be fine, but she wasn't comfortable with the idea.

She stepped away from the window and rolled her shoulders. Maybe it was because she was not doing anything that was making her feel so unsettled. She didn't often have down time. Normally she was focused on the next mission or the next goal. Just hanging around waiting hadn't really been much of a part of her daily life in the last couple months.

She smiled, remembering a conversation with David before Molly had been born. He'd told her she needed to learn to relax.

They'd been sitting on loungers out back of Ileana's house on the estate. They'd only been sitting for about five minutes before Nola bolted to her feet. "You want to do something? Take a walk? Go for a swim?"

David reached out and grabbed her hand, pulling her toward him. She didn't resist and took a seat in his lap, wrapping her arms around him.

He nuzzled her neck. "You need to learn to relax, Nola. Just enjoy the moment. You don't always need to be looking for the next moment. Right now, neither of us has any work to do. The baby's not due for another six months. Let's just enjoy the peace, okay?"

Nola sighed, leaning her head into David's. "I'm not very good at that."

David chuckled, his chest jiggling with the effort. "Oh, I know. I know."

Nola smiled at the memory. And with a shock, she realized she didn't feel sadness at the memory of David. She felt . . . she wasn't sure what exactly she felt. Not joy, but the memory of him didn't make her sad. It made her want to smile. She didn't look too deep into that feeling. She just appreciated that it was finally there.

Her phone rang. She picked it up, unsurprised to see Bishop's name across the screen. She swore that girl was part psychic. She really seemed to know when something was going on with Nola.

"Okay, Bishop—"

"You need to get them out of there now."

Nola didn't waste any time. She headed for the door to the cabin. "Why? What's going on?"

"The new handler. He had you on video along with a file of your known contacts, including Darrin's place. Anyone could access it. It took me five minutes. I can't promise it, but I think the cartel may know where you are. And if they don't yet, they will soon."

Nola winced as she opened the door and hurried inside. Rafe's and Darrin's heads jerked up at her sudden entrance. "We need to move now."

Rafe didn't ask any questions. He grabbed Sofia's hand and pulled her toward the front door. He picked up Enzo and carried him.

Fear slashed across Darrin's face.

"You need to call the cops and get them out here. They've traced us." She gave him a nod and then hurried outside. Pulling her keys from the pocket of her jeans, she unlocked the Bronco.

Rafe was right behind her. He tossed Enzo in the back before picking Sofia up and doing the same. "Put your seatbelt on," he told Sofia as he buckled Enzo's.

Then he ran around the car and jumped into the passenger seat as Nola climbed into the driver's seat and started the car. She had the car moving before Rafe had his seatbelt on.

"Daddy, my seatbelt," Sofia cried.

Rafe turned around over the back of the seat to help Sofia.

Once Rafe had Sofia secure, he turned around and grabbed his own seatbelt, pulling it on.

Nola tore down the road, the Bronco bucking like a real Bronco on the dirt road. The gate was already up as she flew out. Toine stood next to it, looking concerned. Nola said nothing as they raced down the dirt road. It was possible they were ahead of the cartel. Bishop had just discovered the info, and the DA had only recently been assigned.

But in her gut, she didn't think that was true.

Finally, they pulled out onto a paved road, and Nola hit the gas, heading for the LIE.

"What happened?" Rafe asked.

"My source thinks it's possible the cartel knows where we are. The attorney we're supposed to meet tomorrow left the information on his personal computer." Nola quickly pulled onto the LIE. She merged into the traffic heading west.

Nola realized as soon as she pulled onto the LIE that she'd made a mistake. She'd taken her own truck. Her truck felt like it had a neon sign on it. It didn't exactly blend in. Plus, it wasn't the fastest car on the road. Avad had made some changes to the engine, so it definitely was faster than most Broncos. But the Bronco's body was heavy, which limited what the engine could do.

Stupid. She should have taken one of Darrin's instead. But it was too late for that now. She lowered her voice, nodding toward the glove compartment. "In there."

Rafe opened the glove compartment and pulled out the gun case.

It was a Browning. There were ten bullets in the magazine. "You're familiar with it?"

Rafe quickly pulled the gun from the case. He slid the magazine into it with a click and chambered a round. "Yes."

Nola nodded. "Good."

Nola hit the gas as she shifted over to the middle lane. She didn't want to be on the LIE for long. But Wading River was not a very populated area. She needed to get somewhere that they could hold out until Rafe could make it to the meeting in the morning, assuming they were even going. She knew Bishop would be running security scans, and Nola seriously doubted she would be bringing the Ortiz family in tomorrow morning.

But right now, tomorrow morning's meeting was the least of her concerns. Her mind scrambled, trying to figure out some options. There had to be somewhere they could go.

As she drove, she kept an eye on the rearview mirror, looking for any sign of a tail. Behind them, a silver Acura MDX shifted lanes, picking up speed as it came up on their left. Nola watched it, trying to figure out if it was just some guy in a rush or if they were in trouble.

Nola shifted to the right lane, getting one lane in between them. The Acura blew by, an older woman behind the wheel. She didn't even glance at the Bronco before zooming out of sight.

Nola let out a breath. Next to her, she heard Rafe exhale as well, watching the same car. For ten minutes, they drove along the LIE. Nola kept an eye on the rearview mirror, but nothing seemed out of place. And then at William Floyd Parkway, a new shiny red Ford Mustang pulled onto the highway. The Mustang quickly merged into the traffic behind them. Nola watched as the car slowly gained on them. The driver was moving aggressively.

"I think we've got some trouble," she said softly. She glanced into the backseat. "I need you two to put your heads down, okay? Hands over your heads."

"Daddy?" Sofia asked, her voice trembling.

"It's okay, honey. Just do what Nola says, okay?"

Sofia slowly lowered her head. Enzo immediately dropped his head into his lap, putting his hands over it. Ahead was the exit for North Ocean Avenue.

Nola didn't know the area well, but she knew it wasn't one of the main business districts. Which was good, because the last thing they needed was to get caught in a traffic jam at some shopping mall.

But hopefully there would be somewhere that they could get lost. Because there was no way the Bronco was going to be able to outdrive a Mustang. The Mustang pulled closer. Nola stayed in the middle lane, waiting until the last possible second. She jerked the wheel to the right, cutting off a minivan that slammed on its brakes while honking its horn.

She sped across the lanes and onto the exit ramp. The Mustang slammed on its brakes, having bypassed the exit. It started to reverse, ignoring screams of horns and the desperate attempts of people to get out of its way.

Nola yanked on the steering wheel as she made a hard left. The car's wheels lifted up for a second and then bounced back down. In the backseat, Sofia let out a little cry. Nola flicked a glance in the rearview mirror. Enzo sat clutching Sofia's hand, but his gaze stayed focused and directed on Nola. She gave him a nod, turning her attention back to the road.

They were in some sort of business district. Or it had once been a business district. It looked like most of the area had been abandoned a few years earlier. There were still a couple of storefronts holding on, though. They passed a hardware store, a bar, and a locksmith. Beyond them were small homes that looked like they were between a thousand and fifteen hundred square feet.

Which meant even on Long Island they had to cost somewhere upwards of $300,000.

She didn't dart down any of the small roads that branched off the main road. The neighborhoods on those roads wouldn't offer them anywhere to lose their pursuers. Instead, she kept her foot on the gas and prayed that something appeared somewhere along the route.

"There!" Rafe pointed up the road to where there was a series of warehouses.

It looked like the one at the front was still in operation, but the rest looked like they were abandoned. She couldn't tell from here how many there were. She could see at least five. But it was better than nothing. The Mustang had nearly caught up with them by the time she wrenched the wheel to the right and turned into the warehouse area.

Once again, the Mustang overshot them before slamming on its brakes. Nola quickly ducked down the small road between the first and second warehouses on the left. She pulled into the warehouse on her right-hand side, which had its large cargo doors wide open. The building was bare bones, really just a skeleton. It offered nothing.

The door on the other side was open as well. She sped through it, making a sharp left and then another right to cut around a former food warehouse.

"Black duffel bag behind my seat," she said to Rafe.

He reached back and grabbed it.

"There are two bulletproof vests in there. Get them on the kids. There's a phone in there too, in the side pocket. Take it."

Rafe's gaze jerked toward her for a second before he nodded. He pulled out the vests and then tossed the duffel bag on the floor again. He handed one to Sofia and placed the other one on Enzo's lap. "Guys, take your seatbelts off. Sofia, pull that over your head."

Nola tried to keep the car steady as Rafe climbed into the back. A flash of red, and then the Mustang was on the road behind her. She gripped the steering wheel. There wasn't a lot around them. A spot of green appeared behind the Mustang. A Dodge Durango took the turn, quickly speeding up just behind the Mustang.

"There's a second car," Nola said softly.

Rafe shot a quick glance at the back window. He cursed softly under his breath.

Nola quickly sped around the warehouse. There was a small man-made lake beyond the next warehouse. From the corner of her eye, she could see that the Durango was hurrying down the path in between the warehouses. One of the doors of the warehouse was open. She yanked on the wheel and drove up the loading dock and through the heavy plastic strips separating the dock from the larger warehouse itself.

This warehouse wasn't empty. There were pallets filled with empty shipping containers everywhere. The warehouse was three stories high and had a catwalk along each of the second and third floors, the center empty. Nola slammed on the brakes as the Mustang drove by the outside of the warehouse. The Durango drove by on the other side.

"Everybody out." Nola jumped out of the car. She grabbed the back passenger door, pulling it open. She grabbed Enzo, pulling him into her arms. Rafe and Sofia scrambled out the other side of the car.

Nola nodded toward the stairs. "Higher ground."

Rafe had Sofia in his arms, and the two of them sprinted for the stairs. Nola bolted up the stairs, her arms wrapped around Enzo. His arms were clutched around Nola's neck, his head tucked into her shoulder. She could feel his heart pounding away.

He will not be hurt. He will not be hurt, she promised herself as she sprinted up the stairs.

The second floor of the warehouse was only about twenty feet wide and thirty feet deep. Crates lined the space, and there was a small glass-enclosed office at the back. She placed Enzo on the ground. Rafe stopped and looked at her. "What are you doing?"

"Take the kids into the back. Find a hiding spot. There's one number saved on that phone that I gave you. If things go badly, call the number. It'll put you in touch with Bishop. You can trust her."

Rafe's mouth fell open, and he shook his head. "No. I'll—"

"The kids come first, remember? Now go."

Rafe looked like he was about to argue. But then from downstairs came the unmistakable sound of voices. He gave her a nod.

He picked up Enzo and ran with both kids toward the back of the building.

Enzo's hands clutched his father's shoulders as Rafe raced to the back of the floor. But the little boy's gaze stayed on Nola the whole time.

CHAPTER TWENTY-NINE

RAFE

RAFE HURRIED to the office at the back of the second floor. A thin catwalk rimmed the open space to their left. The office had glass windows and no door. Rafe didn't like that, so he had the kids hunker down in the corner of the building, pulling some pallets in front of them. There was a fire ladder outside the window leading downstairs. Worst-case scenario, that would be their exit. It was narrow, which meant if anyone came up, they'd have to do so one at a time.

He carefully grabbed a couple more boxes and placed them in front of the kids, trying not to make too much noise. Sofia sat shaking, her arms wrapped around Enzo. Rafe watched them, his heart breaking. After all they had been through, it could not end like this.

At the same time, he cursed himself. He should've just gone along with the program. Or he should've quit. He'd brought all this down on his family. Mariana was already gone. And he knew he couldn't watch his kids be taken from him too.

Or watch his kids' faces as he was taken from them.

He looked over his shoulder. He could no longer see Nola. She'd hidden herself somewhere. For a moment, he worried that maybe she had left them. But he immediately discounted the idea. He didn't know her very well, but he knew commitment when he saw it. She wouldn't leave them to the vultures downstairs. She would stand in front of them until her last breath.

But he felt like he should be the one offering to be the sacrificial lamb. He felt guilty for that as well. God, he felt guilty for everything these days.

Carefully, he climbed behind the boxes and pulled the Browning out. He had ten shots. And he knew Nola only had four magazines. This was not a good setup.

And if they called the cops, well, the cops might just join the gunmen downstairs. After all, he was still wanted by them. It was such a quagmire. He didn't know how he was going to get out of it.

Or maybe he should say *if* he was going to get out of it.

CHAPTER THIRTY

NOLA

THE ORTIZ FAMILY disappeared into the shadows of the warehouse. Nola rolled her shoulders and then her neck as if shaking off her emotions and concerns.

She was ready.

There were two cars, which meant at least two individuals, most likely more. She had only four magazines, which meant she was going to have to take some of these guys out quietly.

She didn't think this was MS-13. The cars were too nice. But she supposed she'd have to wait and see when they came up the stairs.

She didn't have long to wait. Footsteps sounded on the stairs only a moment later. They were quiet, someone taking their time rather than rushing up.

Nola moved back into the shadows, pulling up her hood as

she hunkered down behind some pallets. She slipped her knife from its sheath. She didn't want a gunfight up here if she could avoid it.

The first man who appeared had blond hair, dark jeans, and a black T-shirt. In his hands was a Glock. He walked up the stairs followed by a second man who was African American and a little older. It looked like he was carrying a CZ 75B SP-01. Neither had any noticeable tattoos and both wore lightweight dark T-shirts. The blond guy's was navy with a noticeable monogram on the right pocket.

The cartel, then.

The men stepped onto the floor. The floor creaked in response. Nola waited until the blond man had passed. The second man stepped on the floor. He paused, scanning the area. Nola held her breath.

Sensing nothing, he moved forward as well, his gun leading the way.

Nola waited until his back was to her, and then she leapt from her spot, her knife clutched in her hand. She slammed a sidekick into the small of his back.

As he arched back, she grabbed onto the back of his shirt and plunged her knife into his throat. He let out a strangled scream, pulling the trigger on his gun in response. The man in front of him whirled around.

Using her guy as a shield, she ran him forward, slipping her hand over the man's hand, and pulled the trigger. Three shots angled across the blond man's chest. He screamed as well and then went down.

Nola yanked her knife out of the throat of the man she held, and let him drop. He crashed to his knees, grabbing for his throat. Nola wrenched the gun from his hand, walked quickly over to the other man, and kicked his gun away. She grabbed his gun and tucked it into her waistband and then wiped her knife on his shirt before sliding it back into the sheath on her side.

He was alive, but unless he got help soon, he wouldn't be for much longer. And being he came here to kill a man and his family for money, she certainly wasn't going to be the one calling for it.

CHAPTER THIRTY-ONE

RAFE

RAFE PEERED around the side of the pallet but couldn't make out anything from where he was. He shifted a little to his right and managed to see part of the stairs just as one of the men stepped onto the landing.

"No more bad men," Sofia mumbled, her hands over her ears.

"It's okay, Sofia, it's okay," Rafe said quietly, only daring to flick a glance at her. She was shaking so hard.

The second man stepped onto the landing and disappeared from view.

A yell sounded, followed almost immediately by gunfire. Rafe's heart pounded. But both the yells had been male.

"No more!" Sofia yelled.

Rafe turned around as Sofia scrambled out around the pallets.

"Sofia, no!" He reached for her, but she slipped out of his grip.

CHAPTER THIRTY-TWO

NOLA

NOLA RIFLED through the pockets of both of the gunmen. She came up with a set of keys in the blonde's pocket and slipped them into her pocket.

A yell sounded from the back of the warehouse floor. Nola's head darted up as a small figure darted in between the pallets.

Sofia.

Nola jumped to her feet as Sofia reached the edge of the floor. Her whole body was shaking, her eyes wide, her face pale.

Rafe darted after her.

Nola shot forward, noticing movement from the other side of the catwalk. Another man had climbed along the edge of the catwalk without being seen. He raised his gun.

Nola sprinted for Sofia. "No!"

From the corner of her eye, she saw the fear slash across Rafe's face. But she was closer.

She put on a burst of speed just as the sound of bullets rang out. The bullets slammed into the ground toward Sofia. Sofia cried out, backing away toward the edge.

Nola dove forward as Sofia toppled. She wrapped her arms around Sofia as the two of them tumbled over the edge into open space.

CHAPTER THIRTY-THREE

RAFE

EVERYTHING SEEMED TO SLOW DOWN. He watched in horror as the man lined Sofia up in his shot. Rafe raised his gun, but he knew he wouldn't be able to take the shot in time. And then Nola was moving. She sprinted across the open space. The shots dotted along the ground, making a beeline for Sofia. Nola tackled Sofia, wrapping her arms around her, and the two of them plunged over the side.

Rafe let out a yell of terror and rage as he shot toward the man's hiding spot. He emptied his clip. The man slumped forward, dead, his gun slipping from his hands as he too plunged to the ground below.

"Enzo, come here!" he called out.

But Enzo stayed where he was, his eyes impossibly large. Rafe sprinted over to him and grabbed him, heading for the stairs. He stopped and grabbed one of the discarded weapons from the other downed men before bolting down the stairs, his heart hammering away.

Please be alive. Please be alive, he prayed silently.

He reached the base of the stairs as more gunshots rang out from his right. He dove with Enzo to the left. The stairs blocked his view of the warehouse floor where Sofia and Nola had fallen. Upstairs, he hadn't looked over the edge to see them. He knew if he saw them lying there lifeless, he just wouldn't be able to handle it.

But now he desperately needed to see that they were all right. But there were two gunmen across the room firing on his position.

The fact that they were firing at him and Enzo and ignoring Nola and Sofia made his heart twist. He looked down at Enzo, who clung to him. He needed to get him to safety.

He pictured Sofia. *Forgive me.*

One of the gunmen moved closer. He'd be on the two of them any moment. The door leading outside was to his left, but still he hesitated. A bullet pinged off the stairs near his head. He ducked down as he sprinted for the door and crashed through it just as another car came around the side of the warehouse and sped toward them.

Damn it. Holding Enzo close, he sprinted across the small roadway to the other warehouse across the way and disappeared inside.

CHAPTER THIRTY-FOUR

NOLA

"MOMMY, WAKE UP! WAKE UP, MOMMY!"

Nola stirred, feeling hands on her. She flicked open her eyes, seeing Molly with her dark hair crouched down next to her, pushing on her shoulder. "Molly?"

"Nola, wake up. Wake up."

Nola's vision cleared. Sofia sat crouched down next to her, tears running down her cheeks.

Then it all came back to her. Sofia on the edge of the floor, Nola grabbing on to her as the two went over. She'd managed to twist in the air, pulling Sofia on top of her as they crashed into a set of wooden pallets. Luckily there had been some heavy cotton packing blankets in between, or Nola would likely be dead.

Right now, though, she was in pain. Her back ached, and her neck was in agony. Her vision swam for a moment. She took a breath and then pushed herself up. The world swayed. She held still for a moment while she gave her body a moment to adjust.

With a groan, she pushed away the broken pallets around them. She rolled off the wooden platform and onto the floor with a thud.

Oh God, everything hurts.

"Nola?"

Nola swallowed, licking her lips. "I'm okay. Where are the men with the guns?"

"They left. They went after Papa."

Nola nodded when she got to her knees and to her feet. Her Browning was three feet away. She grabbed it, scanning the area. The gun she'd taken off one of the men upstairs was God knew where. "Do you know where your dad went?"

Her chest was heaving, tears still rolling down her cheeks, Sofia pointed toward the door they'd come in. "Over there."

Nola stood up with a wince. "Okay. Stay behind me, all right?"

Sofia nodded and then moved to Nola's back.

Nola blinked a few times, her thoughts still a little fuzzy. She was pretty sure she had blacked out for moment there. Her back really ached from where she'd hit, and breathing was not exactly enjoyable right now.

But she'd been in worse shape than this before. She took shallow breaths, calling up her own personal mantra: *You can feel the pain later. Do the job.*

She raised her weapon and scanned the area again. There was no sign of Rafe and Enzo, and everything was quiet.

They had been upstairs when Nola and Sofia had fallen. But there were no sounds coming from the warehouse now. That meant Rafe and Enzo had been chased out or . . .

She didn't want to think about the alternative.

With Sofia tucked in beside her, she made her way toward the stairs. Still no sounds.

Then gunfire sounded from one building over. Relief flowed through Nola. In this case, gunshots were a good sign. It meant Rafe and Enzo were still being pursued.

Making sure to check the corners, Nola hurried toward the door. Sofia stayed right behind her. They reached the exterior door. Nola pushed Sofia back against the wall as she peered outside. There was a white Honda Civic parked across the way at the next warehouse. That must be where the extra guys had come from.

One of those men stood outside the door of the other warehouse. He glanced around occasionally but kept most of his attention on the door.

He was of average height, wearing jeans, a gray thermal top, and a navy-blue vest. Honestly, he could be mistaken for a soccer dad if not for the handgun.

More gunfire came from the other warehouse.

The soccer dad repositioned himself closer to the door, trying to peer through the small dirty window. Nola glanced back down at Sofia. "Just stay here for just a second, okay?"

Sofia shook her head, tears pooling in her eyes. She grabbed Nola's hand.

Nola knelt down and looked into her eyes. "I will not leave you behind. I just need to take care of this one bad guy. Then you and I will go get your dad and Enzo, okay?"

Sofia nodded, even as a tear rolled down her cheek. She stood trembling, and Nola knew there was nothing she could do to stop the poor girl's fear but to make sure that the men responsible for that fear stopped breathing. She stood, a cold resolve falling over her.

Carefully, Nola pulled open the door, thankful when it didn't squeak.

Across the way, the man didn't notice, his attention entirely directed at the building in front of him. Nola propped her hand along the doorframe as she lined up her shot. Amateur.

Nola braced her arms and let out two shots. Both entered the center of the man's back. The man fell forward. Nola waited, but no one responded to her shots.

"Sofia, let's go."

Sofia darted out the door behind her.

"Grab the back of my shirt, but keep your eyes closed, okay?"

Sofia did as she was ordered. Nola crossed the lane, careful to keep her steps slow so Sofia could stay with her. She passed the man that she'd taken down and kicked his gun away. "Keep 'em closed. You're doing great."

She flattened herself against the building. Propping the door open, she glanced inside just as Sofia tried to peer around her. She pushed her back. "Eyes closed."

Rafe slid out from the side of the desk and caught a gunman in the leg. The man screamed and dropped down to the other knee. Rafe put four more slugs into him. The man fell back and went silent.

Nola scanned the room but didn't see anyone else. She waited a heartbeat but didn't hear anyone else either.

Rafe scanned the area, his gun pointed in her direction.

One hand holding Sofia back, she called out, "It's Nola. You clear?"

"Clear," came the call from inside. Nola pulled Sofia in with her, careful to check the corners, but there was no movement. Slowly, she lowered her gun.

Sofia sprinted across the space, wrapping her arms around her father's waist as Rafe stood up from behind the desk. Enzo hugged Rafe's legs. Nola scanned all three of them but didn't see any serious injuries except for a few cuts and abrasions.

"Okay. Let's get moving."

CHAPTER THIRTY-FIVE

NOLA

NOLA'S HEAD and back pounded, but she didn't have time to focus on it. She and Rafe hustled the kids out of the warehouse after Nola made sure the area was clear. Neither of the kids seemed inclined to let go of Rafe anytime soon.

Nola had them walk on the outside of the warehouse to make sure there was no one else inside. The Dodge Durango was parked in front of the opening where she'd driven the Bronco through. Nola pulled out the keys she'd grabbed and pushed on the key fob. The lights blinked as the SUV's locks released.

In the corner of the front windshield was a sticker from a well-known car rental agency. Nola paused and then glanced back at Rafe. "Keep an eye out."

She slid underneath the car, looking around for the GPS tracker. Spying it on the inside of the back bumper, she yanked it off. Pulling herself from underneath the car, she dropped the

GPS and stomped on it. It shattered. She wiped her hands off on her jeans.

At Rafe's raised eyebrows, she said, "They know my car. We need to take something else. This is a rental. It will take them a little while to realize the car's missing. When they do, they won't be able to track it too easily."

He nodded. "Okay."

She gestured to the warehouse. "I need to get my bag from my Bronco, and then we'll—"

"I'll get it."

Before she could say another word, Rafe detangled himself from the kids and disappeared into the warehouse.

Nola stared after him in surprise but then quickly turned her attention back to the two kids. "Okay, you two, let's get you loaded up."

She opened up the back door of the Durango, and Sofia scampered in. Nola turned to Enzo and picked him up to put him in. Before she could release him, he dropped his arms tightly around her neck. "Are the bad men gone?" he whispered into her shoulder.

She rested her hand on his back and leaned her head into his for a moment. "Yes. The bad men are gone."

She placed him in the backseat of the Durango and carefully buckled the seatbelt over him. Then she ran a hand over his face. She wanted to tell him it was safe. She wanted to tell him that everything would be all right. But she knew that was a lie. Everything wasn't all right, at least not yet.

But she promised herself that she would make sure that this little boy and his sister didn't have to fear any more of this. She would find a way to keep them safe.

CHAPTER THIRTY-SIX

RAFE

RAFE HURRIED INTO THE WAREHOUSE. Nola's Bronco sat twenty feet away. He opened the back door and reached in with a shaking hand to grab the black duffel. He pulled it out and then ran a hand over his face.

He'd almost lost them. His legs turned to Jell-O, and he leaned hard against the side of the truck. *Oh my God. I almost lost them.*

If Nola hadn't been there . . .

He pictured Sofia out in the open again. The gunman raising his arm. And then Nola was there, wrapping her arms around Sofia and plunging through the air.

He winced, picturing what the landing must have been like. But they were all right, even Nola, who'd no doubt taken the brunt of the fall. From the angle she'd hit Sofia, Nola should have landed on her. Yet Sofia looked unharmed. Nola, however, walked stiffly. Even while falling, she'd had the strength and presence of mind to somehow maneuver Sofia on top of her.

He swallowed hard. How many times would she save their lives? If Nola hadn't been there, if she hadn't found them, they'd be dead already.

He took a breath, trying to calm his racing heart. He'd known that Nola was surprised when he offered to go get her bag, but he needed this moment to just breathe. Because he was having trouble looking at his kids without wanting to hug them tight and never let them go. But that would only scare them. So he needed to give himself a moment to pull himself together.

He took a seat on the ground, rubbed his hands over his face again, and then shook it off. That was it. That was all he would give himself. That one little moment to feel all of the fear and pain and terror of the last couple of days. Because his kids needed him. And he needed to be there for them.

CHAPTER THIRTY-SEVEN

NOLA

NOLA HAD the car started by the time Rafe reappeared from the warehouse. He went to go put the duffel in the car, but Nola shook her head. "I'll take it."

He handed it over. Nola unzipped the bag and pulled out a baseball cap. She pulled her hair back into a low ponytail at the base of her neck and then slipped the cap over her head. She zipped up her sweatshirt and pulled the hood over the cap. Then she grabbed a pair of sunglasses from inside the bag as well.

Grabbing the bottle of ibuprofen and a bottle of water, she zipped it back up and placed it on the floor behind her seat. Flipping off the lid of the ibuprofen, she downed two with a swig of water. Then she looked at Rafe.

"I think it would be best if you stayed in the back with the kids. They don't know this car, or at least, they're not looking for it yet. But they are looking for a man and a woman. So I think it's best if, at least until we get across the bridges, I'm the only one in the front."

Rafe stared at her. "Are you okay? You took a pretty good fall."

Nola's head seemed to pound harder in response to the question. "I'm good. We're heading down south toward DC. I know a place where they'll be safe."

Rafe nodded. He climbed into the back, sitting in between the two kids. The two kids immediately curled up into his sides. Nola adjusted the rearview mirror and the side mirrors before putting the car into gear. Flicking one last glance at the family whose safety was now her number one priority, she pulled away.

She had planned on taking the family on an extended car trip, but plans had changed. She needed help. And there was only one group of people she trusted for that.

They had an almost-full tank of gas, which was good, as it should hopefully get them at least through the bridges, as long as there wasn't some major traffic jam.

With the state of the bridges off Long Island, however, that was definitely not a guarantee.

Once again, Nola found herself on the LIE, this time heading west. She flipped to 1010 WINS waiting for the traffic report to figure out which bridge would allow her to get off the island the fastest.

She ended up taking the Throgs Neck again, followed by George Washington. And shockingly, the Cross Bronx had not been bumper to bumper, so they actually made it off the island in about an hour. She'd taken the E-Zpass that had been on the car and left it back at the warehouse as well, so she had to slip into the Cash Only lane. She knew that someone would be taking her picture at the tolls, but there was no help for it.

She took the 95, heading south, and felt her body relax a little bit at being out of the Long Island area.

At least here she wasn't imprisoned by water on all sides, making escape impossible.

A glance in the rearview mirror told her that the Ortiz family had fallen asleep.

Nola stretched out her legs and rolled her neck. She could use a nap herself. But she could sleep later. She was used to getting by on very little sleep. But the last few days were definitely pushing her to her limit.

Maybe I'm getting old, she thought.

She would be thirty-seven this year. She'd been in this life since she was sixteen. It was hard to imagine that it had been over two decades now.

She knew that Ileana and Bishop worried about her. But Nola also knew that in order to come back to the land of the living, she had to make sure that what happened to her didn't happen to anyone else. She had to make sure that some people had a guardian angel, even if that guardian angel was incredibly flawed.

She spent the next hour just trudging through her thoughts. It had been a long couple of years. Maybe a little too long.

Sofia had her head in her father's lap, her hair covering her face. And for just a moment, just like back at the warehouse, she could have been Molly.

CHAPTER THIRTY-EIGHT

RAFE

THE ROCKING OF THE CAR, the adrenaline crash, and the two small bodies snuggled next to him were more potent than a sleeping pill. Despite the fact that he'd told himself he needed to stay awake, he was gone before they crossed the first bridge.

Now he stretched his back, his whole body feeling sore. Both kids were still fast asleep. A glance out the window didn't help him identify where they were. Beyond the car was simply a generic highway.

Nola sat behind the wheel. She'd flicked a glance at him when his eyes first opened and then returned her attention to the road.

Carefully, he leaned forward. "How long was I out?"

"About three hours."

"Any problems?"

"Nope. Smooth sailing so far."

He spotted a sign for a rest stop coming up in just a mile and a half. "How about if I drive for a bit?"

Nola nodded. "Okay."

He'd expected her to turn him down. He frowned, worried she was hurt more than she was letting on.

She pulled into the rest stop, choosing a parking spot well away from any other cars. As she stepped out, he carefully let himself out past Enzo.

Enzo stirred, his lids flicking open slightly.

"It's okay. Go back to sleep." Rafe kissed him on the forehead. Enzo's eyes drooped shut again.

As he settled in the driver's seat, Nola pulled the bill of her cap down and leaned against the door. "Just keep heading south toward Baltimore."

She was looking a little paler than Rafe liked. And he knew that she'd hit her head pretty hard. But she didn't complain. He thought about Mariana and how she complained if she got a paper cut. Meanwhile, Nola had fallen a full story and had barely let it slow her down.

"Got it." He put the car into gear. By the time he pulled onto the highway, her eyes were closed, her breathing even.

He drove for ninety minutes, grateful for the silence. It was strange. He'd been on edge for a year. Now, his nightmare had come true. And yet for some reason, on this drive, in this stolen car, he felt the most relaxed and at peace than he could remember. It was almost as if the car had magical abilities that protected him from all the worry and fear, a little oasis of calm.

Or maybe it was the woman in the passenger seat, who he knew would risk her life just as he would for his children.

The gas gauge was at about a quarter tank, and Rafe knew he needed to fill up soon. He couldn't stop at any of the major chains along the highway. Too many cameras. He needed some old out-of-the-way gas station.

He finally spied a small sign for Artie's Gas when he was about thirty minutes outside of Baltimore. He put on his indicator and slipped into the exit lane.

Nola stirred from the passenger seat, looking up groggily. "Where . . ."

"It's okay. It's just a gas station. We're running low."

Her eyes opened as she scanned the gas station. "Any cars following us?"

"Nope. I made sure. We're in the clear."

The gas station must've met her approval because she let her eyes close again.

The gas station looked like it had been built in the 1970s and had never been updated. The gas pumps were still the old kind with the numbers that turned on a wheel.

Rafe popped the gas cover and quickly filled up. He had to go inside to pay. The teenager behind the counter barely looked up.

Rafe grabbed two coffees and paid for them as well. He hurried back out to the car and placed the coffees in the cupholders between the front seat. Nola was in a deep sleep.

He'd gotten her a black coffee. She seemed like the black-coffee type.

He pulled back onto the highway just a few minutes later, his coffee reviving him.

Nola said they were heading to a friend's.

If the friend was anything like Darrin, then he thought they were in good shape. He glanced over at her in the passenger seat. He didn't want to wake her. She'd been through so much already. And not just in the last couple of hours.

She had risked everything to protect his family. When she'd gone through that floor with Sofia, his heart had stopped. But she had saved his little girl. She had put her life on the line to protect his children. She didn't even know them, and yet she didn't hesitate to protect them. She was a rare woman, one who had the skills to back up her desire to help people.

Rafe appreciated every single thing she had done for them. But at the same time, he wanted Nola to find a little peace. To have someone maybe protect her for a change so it wasn't always her body that was on the line.

Not that he thought she'd let him or anyone else do that for her.

But he could at least let her sleep. So he continued driving down the road while Nola slept in the seat next him and his two children slept safely in the backseat thanks to the woman he'd only met twenty-four hours ago.

CHAPTER THIRTY-NINE

NOLA

THE MOVEMENT of the car lulled Nola into a deep sleep. She awoke at the gas station, but sleep pulled her back. She closed her eyes and was lost to the darkness again.

Now she sat on the beach next to David watching Molly play in the surf.

David touched her shoulder with his own. "It's okay, you know."

Nola looked over at him in confusion. "What's okay?"

"To care about other people. You're not replacing us."

"What are you talking about?"

"You know. Rafe and his family. They need you. It's okay to need them back."

Nola shook her head, but David simply nodded toward the water.

Nola turned her head slowly. Molly was still there playing,

but she was no longer alone. Enzo and Sofia played in the water with her. Their hands clasped, they sang "Ring Around the Rosie" and then all plopped down into the shallow water with a laugh. Nola watched them, a smile crossing her face.

Her head jerked up as the sky darkened. She scrambled to her feet. Clouds rolled in, covering the sun.

Molly was gone. Sofia and Enzo were now in the water alone. David had disappeared from next to her, and now it was Rafe sitting there.

In the distance, a shape began to form in the water. It rushed toward the shore, forming a giant wave.

Jumping to her feet, Nola sprinted for the water. Rafe was right next to her, running just as fast. But no matter how fast they ran, it seemed like Sofia and Enzo simply got farther away. The wave moved closer and closer, towering above them. The kids played in the shallow water, singing, completely oblivious to death racing toward them.

Nola dug down deep, trying to dredge up some more speed, but she only seemed to get stuck in the sand. She reached out a hand as the wave crested above Enzo and Sofia. "No!"

Nola jolted, her eyes flying open. Her breath came out as little pants. She stared at the windshield as cars zoomed by.

"It's okay. Everything's fine," Rafe said from the driver's seat before turning his attention to the road. "Bad dream?"

Nola simply nodded, straightening up in her chair and stretching her back with a wince as she tried to calm her breathing. "Yeah. Where are we?"

"We just crossed the Maryland border a few miles back. You were really out."

The clock on the dashboard showed that she'd been asleep for over two hours. Nola could barely believe it. She couldn't remember the last time she'd ridden shotgun in a car. She definitely couldn't remember the last time she'd fallen asleep in someone else's presence. She glanced into the backseat. The kids were still out as well.

Rafe nudged his chin toward the cupholders in between the seats. "I got you a coffee back when we stopped for gas. It's black. Probably a little on the cold side now, but . . ." He shrugged.

Nola grabbed the coffee and took a sip. It was definitely edging toward cold. She took another longer sip nonetheless. She needed to clear her head. Her thoughts were feeling fuzzy. She couldn't shake the image of the wave towering over Sofia and Enzo before crashing down on top of the two of them.

"So I headed toward Baltimore like you said. I didn't want to wake you to get more specific directions, but I think I'm going to need them now."

Nola watched as a highway sign drifted past. "A few more miles to go and then we'll get off the highway. It's only about thirty miles from here, actually."

"And it's safe?" Rafe asked.

Nola took another sip of coffee. Nowhere was perfectly safe. But this was as close to that as she could imagine. "Yes, it's safe."

CHAPTER FORTY

BISHOP

BISHOP PACED in front of her monitors. After she called Nola, Nola had ditched her phone. Bishop had expected that. But she'd expected Nola to contact her by now and let her know what was going on. She knew Nola hadn't expected to head out to Long Island after the New Jersey case, but she should have had an extra burner phone with her.

Or maybe there was a worse reason why Nola wasn't calling her. Bishop shoved that idea far away as soon as she had it. No. Nola was fine. Nola was always fine. It didn't matter what the world threw at her. Nola always managed to get out of it. This would be no different.

But Bishop couldn't help but worry. She had created an algorithm to monitor the police channels on Long Island. So far nothing indicated that Nola had been spotted.

Of course, it was entirely possible that whatever had gone

down had happened somewhere where there weren't a lot of people around. She grabbed the phone and called Darrin.

He answered on the second ring. "Bishop?"

"Hey, Darrin. How are you?"

"I'm fine, I'm fine." Bishop had met Darrin a few times when Nola had gone out to visit him before all their lives had been ripped apart.

"Have you heard from Nola? Is everything all right?" Darrin asked.

Bishop's stomach sank. "I was hoping you'd heard from her."

"No, not since she pulled out of here with that family." Darrin paused. "She's changed."

"I know. Losing Molly and David, I don't know if we'll ever get the old Nola back."

"Maybe not exactly the old one, but maybe someone close."

Bishop looked at her monitors, a light blinking in the corner. "Sorry, Darrin. I have to go."

"If you hear anything, will you call me? I just want to know that they're all right. And I have the kids' stuffed animals. I'll keep them safe until, well, just until."

"Thanks. I know Nola will appreciate that. When I find out something, I'll give you a call, okay?"

"Okay. Take care of yourself, Bishop."

"You too, Darrin."

Bishop disconnected the call, fell into her chair, and grabbed the mouse. She immediately brought up the report. It seemed an investor looking to expand his business had been surveying some warehouses in Patchogue, Long Island. And the warehouses were just off North Ocean Avenue from the LIE.

What he discovered was a bloodbath.

There were multiple bodies strewn across two separate warehouses. There weren't a lot of details yet, but the report did note that all of the victims were male.

Bishop sat back in her chair, exhaling and running a hand over her face. Not Nola.

It was possible one of them was the father, so she knew she shouldn't feel relieved, but she was.

She pulled up a map and realized that the warehouse where the bodies had been found was only about forty minutes from Darrin's camp. If she knew Nola, and she did, she was undeniably heading off Long Island. She'd want to go somewhere safe. She'd want to go somewhere familiar.

Bishop started packing up her gear. Nola was going home.

CHAPTER FORTY-ONE

NOLA

ONCE OFF THE HIGHWAY, the homes got larger and more extravagant the farther they drove. The lots had gone from reasonable half-acre to one-acre plots to acres upon acres.

Sofia woke up in the backseat and stared out the window. She nodded toward a large home with animal-shaped hedges. "Is that a park?"

"No, that's where somebody lives," Rafe said.

"Somebody lives there?" Sofia asked, her jaw falling open.

Nola knew how she felt. When she'd first seen these homes, she'd been completely blown away. She had been driving with David. They'd been dating for four months. He'd been bugging her that entire time to meet his mother. Nola had put it off. She'd known Ileana Hamilton for years. First by reputation, and then they'd even worked on a few projects together. She hadn't seen

Ileana in about two years, though, and she wasn't sure what the woman would think about Nola dating her son.

Ileana was a legend in the intelligence field. She had contacts all over the world and an incredible focus. When Ileana was given a job, the job got done. And that was simply all there was to it.

But it wasn't Ileana's reputation that had intimidated her on the car ride or the fact that she was going to be officially introduced as the girlfriend of her son.

No, it had been the estates that they had passed on their way to Ileana's home. Nola had not grown up wealthy, not by any stretch of the human imagination. She even spent some time in foster care. She firmly remembered piling all of her belongings into a garbage bag to go from one home to the next for a four-year stint when her father had been in prison.

She knew nothing about the lives of people who lived in homes like these. She couldn't even imagine what it was like. And as she'd driven these roads the first time, she'd watched David, who looked so comfortable in this environment. Doubts began to creep into her mind. She'd known that they were different. David had laughed at how different they were, embracing the differences.

But as Nola looked at these homes, she'd realized that they weren't just different—they were from two completely different worlds. David had grown up in a world of privilege. Nola had grown up in a world of poverty.

Yet she couldn't lump David in with all the other smug, arrogant wealthy people she'd met in her life. David was the opposite of that. He was a human rights lawyer and had started a charity to help refugees resettle in the United States. He was a good man.

But when she looked at all of these extravagant homes, it was hard to remember that he wasn't one of them.

David reached over and took her hand. "Quit freaking out."

Nola straightened up in her seat. "What? I'm not freaking out."

David took her hand and kissed the back of it. "Oh, yes you are. You're looking at all of these homes, and your rich bias is coming into play. You're doubting that you and I belong together."

"I don't have a rich bias," Nola mumbled.

David laughed out loud. "You are the most anti-wealth person I have ever met. But you know me, and you know my mom. You know we're not like those images you've created in your head."

Nola squirmed, feeling a little unsettled that he had read her so easily. "What if she doesn't approve of you dating me?"

Dave raised an eyebrow at her and gave her a smile full of love. "It's not possible, Nola. Because she'll take one look at my face and know I'm a goner, and that's all she'll care about."

Nola smiled at the memory as she looked out at the houses. "When I first drove down here, I thought the houses were ridiculous too. They seemed almost like castles."

Sofia nodded in the back, her face all but pressed up against the window.

"But the people inside them, they can be good too. Not all of them, of course, but like with anyone else, there's good and there's bad." She nodded to the road coming up. "Make a right here."

Rafe turned on the blinker and turned down the street. There were no homes on this street, just trees and grass on either side with a tall fence surrounding them. The fence had cameras every few feet.

"Do you have that phone?" Nola asked.

Rafe wrestled it from his back pocket and handed it over.

Nola dialed. It was answered quickly. "Yes?"

"Hey, Avad. I'm in the Durango. We'll be at the main house in a few minutes."

"Good. Ileana will be very happy to see you."

"Tell her I'm bringing some guests."

"Bishop already called her to tell her. We'll see you in a few minutes."

Nola shook her head as she put the phone away. Bishop knew her incredibly well. She still wasn't sure if that was a good thing or a bad thing.

They continued for another mile before the forest gave way to a well-manicured lawn. There was a pasture on the left, and three horses grazed within it. One white horse galloped next to the car as if racing Rafe to the end. Enzo, who had woken up at Sofia's squeals of joy, looked out the window, a smile slowly crossing his face.

At the end of the road was a guardhouse. The gate was down, but it immediately raised as they approached. The guard looked into the car and nodded, catching sight of Nola. She knew that he had already taken video of her and Rafe and identified her from the moment they had turned onto the road.

After the pasture was more green grass, and then straight ahead of them was the mansion. It had brown and white stone covering it with white shutters and a side porch on the left-hand side. The house extended out on each side and was two stories high. In front was a circular driveway where a well-manicured hedge encircled a fountain. It looked like a perfect English estate.

Rafe slowed as he drove up. "*This* is a safehouse?"

Nola looked up at the place that currently was as close to a home as she got. "There's no place safer."

CHAPTER FORTY-TWO

RAFE

THE DOORS to the mansion opened. Rafe expected some sort of uniformed butler to step out, but instead it was a woman who looked to be in her late fifties. She had long, thick, dark hair that was pulled back into a bun. She wore a stylish navy-blue dress with matching heels and a colorful red scarf thrown over her shoulders.

Behind her stepped a giant of a man. Tall and muscular with dark-blond hair, he was only a little bit younger than the woman.

"Here's good," Nola said, pointing to right in front of the house. Rafe stopped the car and put it in park.

Nola turned to look at the kids in the backseat. "These are friends of mine. You'll like them," she said before she stepped out of the car.

The older woman smiled at the sight of Nola, holding out her arms. And for the first time, Rafe noticed the acid burn down the side of her neck.

Nola walked up the stairs and let the woman hug her. Then she conferred with the woman for a moment and said something to the man behind her. The man disappeared back into the house as Nola and the woman walked back toward the car.

"Where are we, Papa?" Enzo asked.

"A friend of Nola's. We're going to stay here for a little while I think."

He stepped out of the car. Nola and the woman made their way around toward him. Nola nodded toward the woman. "Rafe, I'd like you to meet Ileana Hamilton, the former Director of National Intelligence."

Rafe felt his heart skip a beat. His gaze shifted from Nola to the woman. The former Director of National Intelligence? Why on earth had Nola brought them here?

The woman seemed to notice his alarm. She extended her hand, and Rafe shook it out of habit. The woman smiled warmly at him. "That is one of my titles. I prefer the title of mother-in-law."

That title didn't provide Rafe with any less shock. If anything, it shocked him even more. Nola was married? The thought had never occurred to him. She definitely seemed like someone who was on her own in the world.

And he tried and failed to ignore the feeling of disappointment that wafted through him at the revelation.

He was also incredibly curious. Was her husband here? He felt strangely jealous, which he knew he had no right to feel.

But he didn't get a chance to say any more as Sofia climbed from the back of the car into the driver's seat and then out the door behind him. "Hi," she said softly.

Rafe shook himself from his surprise. "Um, this is Sofia. Sofia, this is Mrs. Hamilton."

"I'm very pleased to meet you," Ileana said, extending her hand.

Sofia shook it awkwardly. "Nice to meet you too."

Rafe walked to the back of the car and pulled Enzo from inside. He still looked half asleep.

"And this is Enzo," Rafe said as Enzo laid his head on his shoulder.

Ileana's smile grew even warmer. "You have a beautiful family, Rafe. I would be very happy if you would stay with me for a little while as we figure out your situation."

Rafe looked around. It really did look like a house out of *Downtown Abbey*. Mariana would've loved it. "Thank you. I appreciate that."

THE INSIDE of the house was as stunning as the outside of it. The large foyer opened up into a sitting room on one side and a study on the other. Light-colored wide-plank floors ran throughout the house. The walls were a pale gray with bright white trim. Artwork and family pictures dotted the space along with colorful rugs. It all screamed money and yet at the same time was somehow welcoming.

Ileana led them inside, and Avad, who as far as Rafe could tell was some sort of bodyguard-butler combination, showed them up to their rooms. As Rafe walked up the stairs with Sofia and Enzo, his feet sinking into the thick floral rug, he glanced over his shoulder. Ileana had linked her arm through Nola's and was walking with her down the hall.

Rafe turned his attention back to Avad but couldn't help but wonder about the relationship. Ileana obviously cared deeply for Nola. And despite her reticence about hugging, Nola seemed to genuinely like the woman.

Yet Nola had struck him as a loner. Once again he wondered what the backstory was, but knew he had no right to ask.

Avad showed them to a room on the second floor. There was a huge king-size four-poster bed in the middle of the wall opposite the door. A fireplace was across from it, and two chairs sat in front of it.

Avad stepped aside so that they could all enter. "Nola thought that the three of you might want to share a room. I will bring up an extra bed later to accommodate you."

Rafe shook his head. "That won't be necessary. We can all stay in the same bed."

"I'll bring it up anyway. If you don't want to use it, that's all right." Avad nodded toward the door to the side of the bed. "The bathroom's in there. There's fresh towels and all the essentials that you will need. There are clothes in the armoire that should fit you and the children. I had to guess a little on sizes, but I think I did all right."

"You had all this prepared?"

"Ileana is rarely caught off guard. She had a feeling that you would be showing up at some point, so she had everything prepared for you."

Rafe was floored by the idea of it.

Avad grasped the handle. "I will leave you to it. When you're done, just come down the stairs and around the banister. Ileana and Nola will be in the kitchen. Dinner will be served whenever you're ready." Avad closed the door behind him.

Sofia squealed, kicking off her shoes and jumping up on the bed. She bounced up and down on it, a smile on her face. "We really get to sleep here?"

Rafe looked around, not quite believing it himself. "Looks like. Now, how about a bath? I have a feeling there's going to be quite a bathtub in that bathroom."

CHAPTER FORTY-THREE

NOLA

THE FEEL of Ileana's arm through Nola's was both familiar and strange. They stepped into the kitchen.

It was all white with stainless steel appliances. A large island with a waterfall counter of white and gray dominated the space. Next to it, a three-tiered display of fruit sat on the long heavy wooden table alongside pitchers of water and sweat tea, and four glasses.

"Are you thirsty?"

Nola shook her head as she took a seat at the table. What she really wanted was a shower, but she knew she needed to speak with Ileana first. "No, I'm good."

A row of floor-to-ceiling windows and a large set of full glass patio doors lined the back wall, offering a view of the patio and the grounds beyond it.

Ileana sat across from Nola at the kitchen table. Nola steeled herself, knowing that Ileana was busy inventorying every bump and bruise on Nola's body. "It seems like you've had a rough few days."

Nola shrugged. "I've had worse."

Ileana didn't say anything, although Nola knew she was biting her tongue. Ileana supported Nola in her missions. She knew why it was so important to her. But at the same time, more than anything, Ileana wanted Nola to find a less dangerous outlet for her passion. But she never pushed her to stop. That, among many reasons, was why Nola loved her.

Ileana nodded toward the hall. "Like I told Rafe, they are a beautiful family."

"They are. The kids have been through so much. There's a lot of trauma packed into their memories now."

"Early trauma can be incredibly destructive, especially on young minds. But if handled correctly, it can serve as a way to strengthen the child to face whatever the world will throw at them."

Nola knew Ileana spoke from experience. In Afghanistan, her mother had been killed in front of her when she was only six years old. She and her father had fled the warlords and made it to Kabul. There, her father had struggled to make ends meet while Ileana went to school.

Unlike a lot of fathers at the time, he forced his daughter to stay in school even when she wanted to leave to help pay the bills. But he wouldn't hear of it. "Your future, our future, is being created with every fact you learn. The small gain we would get from you leaving school to help out will be greatly offset by the long-term gains we will achieve by your education. You will stay in school, daughter."

Sadly, her father had never lived to see the benefits of his sacrifice.

But Ileana had most definitely made good use of that educa-

tion. She had become a translator with an American corpora-
tion that was actually a CIA front that had come to
Afghanistan in the late eighties. They'd brought her with them
when she left. She was an agent for a decade before switching
over to admin and then going to work for the State Department.
She'd had a number of high-level positions within the intelligence community before she was named the deputy secretary
of state. Her last position was as the Director of National Intelligence.

Nola took a sip of the sweet tea Ileana had poured for her.
"Have you heard anything from Bishop? Do we know what's
going on with the handler?"

"I had my people contact him. I told him we had to postpone
the meeting. And there was an additional benefit to the post-
ponement."

"A new handler?"

Ileana nodded. "Yes. His name is Brent Ackers. He's a much
more seasoned individual. He's been a US attorney for ten years,
but he was with the US Marshal service for nearly the same
amount of time before that. We'll set something up, maybe for
tomorrow, closer to us. In a situation that we can control."

"The cartel is truly out for him. I don't know how we're going
to get him out from under it."

Ileana sighed. "'The belief in a supernatural source of evil is
not necessary; men alone are quite capable of every wickedness.'"

Nola nodded, completely agreeing with the Joseph Conrad
quote.

Down the hall, the front door opened. Bishop's voice rang out
through the first floor. "Ileana? Nola?"

Nola looked up as Bishop burst into the kitchen.

Bishop's energy seemed to crank up all the emotions in the
kitchen an extra few notches. She sprinted over to the table and
wrapped her arms around Nola before Nola could even say a

word. "Oh, thank God. I heard about the warehouse, and I got so worried."

She removed her arms from Nola and then quickly moved to the other side of the table and hugged Ileana. "I told you she would come here."

Ileana patted Bishop's hand. "Yet again, you were right."

Bishop pulled her messenger bag from over her shoulder and placed it on the counter with a heavy thump. Then she pulled out a chair and sat down. "So what's going on? Are the Ortizes here?"

"Yes, they're upstairs getting settled in," Avad said as he walked into the kitchen.

Bishop smiled over at him. "Oh, hey, Avad. What's for dinner?"

Avad walked to the refrigerator. "I marinated some steaks. Everything else is ready. I thought we'd eat outside tonight. I'll put on the burners."

"That sounds great," Bishop said, pouring herself a glass of sweet tea.

Nola found that it did sound good. Even with the chill in the air, the outside burners made the patio feel like spring. She stood up. "Well, if you guys will excuse me, I think I'll go take a shower. I desperately need one."

Ileana stood as well. "Of course, my dear." She walked over and hugged Nola yet again before kissing her on the cheek. "It is good to have you home. No matter how long the visit."

Nola nodded, smiling at her, and then walked out of the kitchen. She had been back to the estate a few times over the last few months. But this was the first time she had surprised them with a visit.

It was the first time she was returning to ask for help.

And it was the first time she didn't see Molly as soon as she stepped into the house.

CHAPTER FORTY-FOUR

BISHOP

BISHOP WATCHED Nola walk out of the room and then immediately turned to Ileana, dropping her voice. "She seems better, right? Don't you think she seems better?"

Ileana retook her seat and patted Bishop's hand. "She seems changed. For the better."

Bishop sat back in her chair. "I bet it's this case. Those kids. I mean, Nola will help anyone who needs help, but helping kids . . . that's got to touch something deep inside of her."

A wistful tone entered Ileana's voice. "And the daughter, she looks a little like Molly."

Bishop's gaze automatically shot to Ileana's face. She had only been thinking about how the resemblance to Molly would effect Nola. She hadn't thought about Ileana and the impact it would have on her. Ileana had adored Molly. Pain was etched across Ileana's face. "I'm so sorry. Are you okay?"

Ileana nodded, her eyes looking a little bright. "For a moment, when she stepped out of the car, I thought . . ." She shook her head. "But that's not important. What's important is that there is another little girl and little boy that need our help. And we're going to do everything we can to help them."

Bishop leaned forward. "The handler said that he could meet with Rafe tomorrow."

"Let's have him come here. I have enough influence that it will not seem so unusual for someone to come ask my advice. I'd like to make sure that everything is under our control as much as possible. I'll have extra security put on the day shift. And I'll call Chandra."

Chandra Wilson was a former intelligence agent who was also a national security lawyer.

Bishop nodded. "I'll stay around too. Just to make sure everything's all right."

"You don't have to lie to me. I know you'll stay here as long as Nola stays."

Bishop shrugged, not meeting Ileana's gaze. "I just like how I feel when she's around. It feels like . . ." Bishop shrugged again.

"It almost feels like before," Ileana said softly.

Bishop nodded. "Yeah, a little."

But Bishop knew it wasn't exactly like before. It would never be like that again. David and Molly dying had fractured their family. Changed it permanently.

But unlike Nola, Bishop wanted to cling to the family she had left. She wanted to be near them as much as possible. If that meant that she simply hung out at Ileana's house for as long as Nola stayed, well, then that was what she was going to do. Because she knew all too well that all she could count on was today. Tomorrow was not guaranteed.

CHAPTER FORTY-FIVE

NOLA

NOLA OPENED the door to her room, unsurprised that every-thing looked the same. Ileana always kept everything exactly as she had left it. There was an antique canopy bed with fluffy white linens positioned above a green, ivory, and blue rug. Long heavy blue drapes hung from ceiling to floor, framing the two large windows that overlooked the garden.

She and David had always stayed in this room. When Molly was little, she had stayed with them as well. But when she'd gotten a little bit older, she insisted on having her own room when she came to visit Nona.

So Ileana had the room next door made up for her. Nola crossed to the door that connected to Molly's room. She hesi-tated, her hand hovering above the handle before she took a breath and opened the door.

Facing her was a little girl's dream. The walls were covered in a muted white wallpaper with small pink rosebuds dotting it. There was a shelf unit shaped like a house that was filled to bursting with stuffed animals. Dolls lined another shelf above the toy chest that from experience Nola knew was filled. The white poster bed had a pink comforter with horses embroidered on it. The rug was a white shag that she and Molly had spent countless hours lying, playing, and just talking on.

It had been two years, but neither Ileana nor Nola had brought up the idea of converting the room.

Molly was nowhere to be seen today. Nola found it odd she hadn't seen her yet. That was extremely unusual. Concerned, she stepped into the room. "Molly?"

The rocking chair in the corner of the room began to move. Molly looked up at Nola with Lulu, her small white dog, in her lap as usual. "Hi, Mommy."

"What are you doing? Were you hiding from me?"

Molly shrugged. "I don't know."

Nola walked across the room. "What's going on? What's wrong?"

Molly shook her head. "I don't want to say."

"It's okay. You can tell me."

Molly took a deep breath and then looked up. "Daddy said he can't see you anymore. That there's somewhere else he has to be."

Nola sucked in a breath but not because David wouldn't be coming to see her anymore. She had realized that a while back when she had simply stopped seeing him. Today in her dream was the first time she'd seen him in months. "But you can still see him, right?"

Molly gave her a look as if she wasn't very bright. Which, when it came to these kinds of issues, Nola fully admitted she wasn't. "Of course. But you can't. Doesn't that make you sad?"

Nola thought about it for a moment and realized that it did

make her sad on one hand, but on the other hand, she knew it was time. "It's just how things are."

"I'm not leaving you."

Nola looked into her daughter's face, the face she loved more than any on this planet, and knew that one day it would be time for Molly to stop coming to see her as well. "Perhaps one day you will. And that will be all right too."

Her heart ached even as she spoke. Losing Molly had been gut-wrenching. She didn't know how she would have survived without these visits. They kept her sane, even as she wondered if maybe the visits were actually proof of the opposite.

"I met Sofia and Enzo's mom. She's very sad. She doesn't understand why she can't be with them."

Once again, Nola didn't know what to say. But Molly continued on. "But it's okay. I told her that you'd look out for them now. And that they would be okay."

Nola felt a lump in her throat at her daughter's faith in her.

"They need your help, Mommy. You need to stay with them."

"I will. Tomorrow their dad is going to meet with a man from the government. And then everything should be fine."

Molly stopped rocking. She looked straight at Nola, seeming much older than her eight years. "It won't be fine, Mommy. It won't."

AFTER MOLLY LEFT, Nola took a long hot shower. Her back ached from where she'd crashed through the pallets. When she stepped from the shower, she took a look at her back in the mirror and winced. The bruises were going to be substantial.

With a sigh, she pulled on a pair of black sweats and a matching T-shirt. Bruises in the grand scheme of things weren't too bad. She knew her rib cage was a little bruised as well, although she was pretty sure it wasn't worse than that.

All in all, she'd been pretty lucky. They all had.

Stepping from the bathroom, she was tempted to climb into bed right now, that's how tired she was. But if she did that, she'd have a heck of a time sleeping tonight no matter how tired she was. So after drying her hair, she headed downstairs.

Ileana was talking on the phone in her study. Avad was working in the kitchen. She made her way to the front hall closet and pulled out her old hiking boots and a heavy fleece jacket. After pulling them on, she slipped out the front door and headed around the side of the house and stepped onto the path that led to the family cemetery.

It was beautiful out, despite the chill in the air. It was always beautiful on the estate, even when it stormed. There was something about the estate that made her feel connected to the people who'd been here before. Or maybe it was just Nola because she could see flickers of them sometimes.

When she was a kid, she often couldn't tell the difference between a ghost and a real person. It made for some difficult situations. Her father hadn't exactly been receptive to the idea, so she learned early on to hide that particular ability.

As she'd gotten older, she'd seen fewer and fewer. Anna Mae's grandmother was the first ghost she'd seen in years that she hadn't known while they were alive. She supposed the more rational part of her brain had taken over and shut down the more whimsical part of her brain that believed in there being more to this life than what was right in front of your face.

But when David and Molly had died, she had turned to that more whimsical side, desperate to see them again if at all possible.

She wasn't sure what to think about David not being able to come back to her now. On the one hand, she knew it was for the best. Once you'd passed on, you shouldn't spend too long on this plane. One day, she would have to help Molly cross over too. Not that she knew how to do that.

A flash of movement caught her attention from the corner of her eye. She had the impression of a white dress and long blonde hair. But when she turned her head, there was no one there.

But she knew what it was, or rather, who it was. Mariana had been keeping an eye on her children. Nola had felt her presence since she had first come across them. She'd seen the vague outline of the woman in the parking lot of the Sayonara Motel first, and then she'd seen her more clearly at Darrin's camp. But unlike Molly, who seemed to accept her present state, Mariana was desperate to return. She was desperate to keep her children safe.

But there was nothing she could do from where she was.

Nola couldn't blame the woman. She supposed she would feel exactly the same if their positions were reversed and it was Molly here on her own.

But then again, Sofia and Enzo still had their father. He was a tough man, a strong man. He'd protected his kids the best he could with what limited resources had. And she really hoped that as time moved on that everything worked out with this government official tomorrow.

It won't be fine, Mommy. It won't.

A chill stole down Nola's back. She shook it off as she opened the gate to the cemetery. It would be all right. Ileana had checked the man out. After tomorrow, hopefully the Ortiz family would be well on their way to a new, safer life.

CHAPTER FORTY-SIX

RAFE

RAFE LEANED his hands against the side of the shower, his head bowed. The water was hot, almost painful, but he made no effort to change it. He needed the heat.

His mind was having a tough time shifting gears. It was difficult to take in all that happened in the last forty-eight hours. He was wanted by the cops. The cartel had managed to send assassins after him and his children. They had been in a shoot-out where he had been convinced for a moment that he had lost his daughter.

And yet they were still here. They were still alive.

It was a damned miracle. And that miracle's name was Nola.

He shut off the water, stepped out of the shower, and grabbed one of the big fluffy towels on a shelf. Ileana had made sure that they had everything to make them feel comfortable. That was also hard to wrap his head around. Nola's mother-in-law was the former Director of National Intelligence. There had to be quite a story behind that fact.

And Nola was married.

That was a completely unexpected revelation as well. She hadn't struck him as someone with those kinds of ties. Of course, he hadn't heard any mention of the husband, although he'd seen a picture of Nola and him downstairs. And then another one of Nola, the same man, and a little girl.

Nola was a mom too. Once again, he struggled to accept the new information. It wasn't that he didn't think she could be a mom. He simply struggled with the idea of a mom going out there and taking on the world the way she did. It was so dangerous.

He toweled off his hair and then slipped on the clothes that Avad had left for them in the armoire. It was sweatpants and a long-sleeved T-shirt. There were even sneakers for each of them.

Rafe wasn't sure what to think about that. He didn't like taking charity or handouts. But in this situation, beggars couldn't be choosers. And right now, they were most certainly beggars.

He stepped out into the room. Sofia and Enzo lay on the end of the bed watching TV. He frowned. There'd been a lot of TV in the last couple months. He glanced out the window. The estate was gorgeous. And apparently it spanned acres and acres. With security surrounding it. He looked back at his kids and clapped his hands. They barely blinked at the movement.

He rolled his eyes as he walked over and turned the TV off.

"Dad," Sofia grumbled.

"That's enough TV. Let's go get some fresh air."

Sofia glanced at the window and then back at her father. "Is it safe?"

"There are guards outside along the perimeter and a big fence. The woman who owns this house is very important. So she has lots of security. Plus, no one knows we're here. So yes, it's safe."

His heart broke at the look of fear on Sofia's face. She glanced toward the window again. "Are you sure?"

"I'm sure. Nola wouldn't have brought us here if it wasn't safe."

Sofia reluctantly rolled off the bed. Rafe helped Enzo tie his shoes while Sofia pulled on hers. Then Rafe grabbed the fleece jackets from inside the closet. Once he had the kids bundled up, they made their way down the stairs.

Avad came out of the kitchen wiping his hands on a towel. "Are you three hungry?"

"Getting there. It smells delicious. I thought I'd take the kids outside for a little fresh air."

Avad waved them on as he headed back to the kitchen. "Come this way. I'll show you the path that leads to the playground."

THE ESTATE WAS lush even though most of the flowers had died off. Rafe recognized some of the bushes and flowerbeds even in their barren state. *It must be spectacular in the spring and summer*, he thought.

They followed the path that Avad had pointed out, and only a few dozen feet from the house, a playground came into view.

Sofia smiled and took a step toward it and then stepped back, looking at her father.

"It's okay. Go ahead," Rafe said.

Sofia grinned and then ran for the slide. Enzo held back for a moment and looked up at Rafe. "Nola?"

Rafe squeezed his son's hand and then got down on one knee so that he could look him in the eyes. "She's around here somewhere. It's okay. If there were any trouble, you know she wouldn't leave you alone."

Enzo nodded and then hurried off after Sofia.

There was a wooden bench set off to the side of the playground, and Rafe made his way over to it.

He sat down and had only been sitting for a few minutes when he spotted Nola walking out of a separate path a hundred yards or so away. She continued on to a small area enclosed by a metal fence. With a start, Rafe realized it was a cemetery.

A young woman appeared down the path that he and the kids had taken. She had wild curly hair and a complexion that attested to a mixed heritage. She smiled warmly at Rafe. "Hi. I'm Bishop."

More surprises. Rafe had heard Nola speaking with Bishop a few times over the last few days, but for some reason he'd expected a man. And someone older. He stood up and extended his hand. "I'm Rafe. Thank you for all of your help."

Bishop blushed and ducked her gaze. "Oh, it's nothing. I mean, it's what I do."

"We really appreciate it."

"I just wanted to introduce myself and let you know that dinner will be ready in about fifteen minutes. Avad sent me down to let you know." She paused, looking around. "I thought Nola would be here with you."

Rafe shook his head, nodding toward the cemetery. "She's over there."

Bishop glanced over her shoulder. "I should've known."

She took a step as if to leave, but Rafe spoke quickly. "Would it be okay if I told her? I wanted to speak with her about something."

Surprise flashed across Bishop's face, and then she nodded. "Sure. Do you want me to stay with the kids?"

"That would be great. Thank you."

He walked to the edge of the playground. "Sofia. Enzo."

Sofia looked up from where she sat at the top of the slide. Enzo was once again playing in the sand. "I'm just going to talk to

Nola for a minute." He pointed out where he'd be. "This is Bishop. She's a friend of Nola's, and she's going to stay with you, okay?"

Sofia darted a glance over at where Nola was and then gave a reluctant nod.

Rafe knew he was going to have to address everything they'd been through in the last couple of days, but now was not the time. He gave Sofia what he really hoped was a reassuring smile and then headed toward the cemetery.

Nola stood with her back toward him as he made his way over. She didn't turn as he entered the cemetery, although he had no doubt that she knew he was there. He came and stood next to her, staring down at the tombstones in front of her. David Hamilton. And Molly Hamilton.

His heart plummeted at the sight, even though he'd suspected it after seeing the pictures. "I'm sorry."

Nola looked up and wiped a tear from her eyes. "It was two years ago. A man who I told the government should be locked up killed them. It was meant for me. But they were the ones who got caught in the blast."

He sucked in breath, feeling the jolt of connection. Mariana had been killed because of him. The kids had been put in danger because of him.

"It's not easy," he said.

"No, it's not."

"So that's when you started this? Helping people?"

Nola nodded. "The system can be very good at times but also very rigid. It doesn't seem to recognize that the bad guys have more resources. And that they can and will exploit the loopholes in the system. And sometimes people just aren't good. So I try to make sure that other people don't have to go through what I went through. Or at least that the perpetrators are brought to justice."

"And what about you? Did you get justice?"

She shrugged. "He was killed by police officers. I suppose that's a form of justice."

"But you wanted to do it yourself."

Nola paused. "I don't know if I wanted to do it myself so much as I wanted to be there to see that he was well and truly dead."

He turned and stared at the graves. "I understand that."

For the first time, Nola turned and looked at him. "I think you do."

"Daddy!" Sofia called.

Rafe turned to look over his shoulder. Sofia was standing at the edge of the playground, waving at him. Enzo stood next to her, his hands behind his back but looking at them.

"Bishop says dinner's ready."

Nola rolled her shoulders as if casting off her mood. "We don't want to keep Avad waiting. He gets a little grumpy when people don't show up on time for his dinners."

Picturing the tall Viking, Rafe gave a small shudder. "I don't think I want to make him angry."

"Oh, you definitely don't. He'll burn your steak." She turned for the gate.

Rafe stepped next to her and held the gate open for her to pass. His gaze caught hers for a moment as she walked by him. That connection he felt when he was near her sprung to life.

Then she looked away and headed toward Bishop and the kids. Rafe once again fell in step with her, noting that the connection he felt for her had deepened another bit with the short conversation.

CHAPTER FORTY-SEVEN

RAFE

DINNER HAD BEEN DELICIOUS. The conversation light and easy. He could see why Ileana had risen through the intelligence ranks. She was smart and insightful. Plus, she managed to wheedle stories and facts from everyone at the table while making it seem like just plain curiosity.

He hadn't realized until after dinner just how much he had shared. He blamed it partly on how tired he was. Once his belly was full, he was having trouble staying awake. The kids were in the same predicament.

So he'd said their good-nights and ushered them upstairs. He tucked the two kids in, and a few minutes later, they were out almost immediately.

Rafe crawled in between them, looking forward to a good night's sleep. Yet when he closed his eyes, his mind seemed to take it as a cue to send all his worries into overdrive. It wasn't because he didn't think the estate was secure. Avad had shown Rafe the security precautions of the estate before they went upstairs for the night. He'd met Avad's brother, Darus, another Viking in appearance, who took over for the night shift, keeping an eye on the estate and making sure everything was running as it should.

Rafe felt better knowing that there were people outside keeping watch. In his gut, he knew no place was ever perfectly safe, but this was definitely a few steps up in the protection sphere. But still sleep eluded him.

The room wasn't helping. It was so big it was hard to feel comfortable. He'd gotten used to small rooms. Now he felt like he was sleeping on a stage. But that wasn't the main reason for his sleeplessness either.

It was the meeting tomorrow.

He knew he would have to hand over the information on the cartel. He'd told his last handler about what he knew, but he'd refused to hand over the evidence until he had an agreement in writing that included lifetime protection for himself and his kids. His handler had tried to get him to hand the information over, promising that the protection was a guarantee. But Rafe had held firm.

Now that his handler was dead, he was glad he had done it that way.

He wasn't sure if this new handler would let him get away with that. But he needed a guarantee of the kids' safety. But what if the new handler refused to play ball? What was he going to do then? It wasn't like he had a lot of options. He needed the government's protection. He would be dead without it.

Rafe sat up and slowly extricated himself from the two kids who were curled up into his sides. It wasn't easy. He had to practically crawl down the middle of the bed to get out. He tucked the blankets back around the two of them and then strode over to the window.

Tomorrow was make-or-break for his little family. Rafe knew he would have to do whatever it took to ensure their safety.

He just wasn't sure if it was going to be enough.

CHAPTER FORTY-EIGHT

NOLA

THE SUN WASN'T EVEN up when Nola stepped out the front door of Ileana's house. She stretched her back a little, wincing at the pain. But she shoved it aside as she headed down the steps. She started off with a slow jog and then gradually increased her pace as she reached the fence line. She knew this path well. If she stayed along the fence, it was just over five miles. She needed the exertion this morning.

The air was crisp, and the tip of her nose quickly got cold. Her cheeks felt almost chapped from the air. But she loved it. It cleared her head, and she needed that.

Rafe and his family would have their lives changed forever today. She and Ileana had spoken into the night, trying to figure out what they would do if the situation fell through with the Ortizes today. Both of them had connections, and they could create fake identities for the family to keep them protected. But it would also keep them illegal. And while that might be okay in the short run, in the long run, that wouldn't be ideal for any of them, especially the kids as they aged.

And the cartel had long memories. They might need that legalization down the road and the protection that would come with it.

Nola hated everything about this situation. Rafe had done the right thing. He had tried to help people. He and his children shouldn't have to pay for the rest of his life for doing the right thing.

But the world did not always reward the well-intended. It seemed more often than not it rewarded those with power.

Nola had made it her mission for the last two years to upset that balance and put it back in favor of those who did right, as well as to punish those who did not. So the idea of the Ortizes having to spend the rest of their lives looking over their shoulders was not acceptable to her.

She would need to figure something out. She just didn't know what it was yet.

As she pounded down the path, she fell into a rhythm with her footfalls. It was a quiet morning. The chill in the air indicated that winter wasn't far off. Nola had always loved how the estate looked in the winter. It was all smooth snow and evergreens sprinkled in white as well. The fireplaces being lit just made it feel so cozy. Like a throwback to yesteryears.

When David had been alive, this estate had felt as comfortable to her as her and David's home. Actually, truth be told, it felt more like home. They'd often switched between the two seamlessly.

A lot of people might not have loved the idea of living with their in-laws, but Nola had found comfort in the routine. Bishop had been with Nola since she was sixteen years old. And she, too, found comfort switching between Ileana's and Nola's home.

In fact, Bishop had only moved out a month before David and Molly were killed. Bishop had stayed over last night as well.

And for the first time since David and Molly had died, Nola had woken up in Ileana's home feeling good. Of course, then she'd immediately felt guilty, as if she didn't deserve to feel good. The rational part of her brain knew that that was just a normal part of the grieving process.

But the fact that, if for even a moment, she felt good seemed a good sign. Maybe she was finally coming through to the other side.

Maybe it was having kids in the house.

Maybe it was Rafe.

But she didn't look too closely at those feelings. She was attracted to him, that was true enough. And understandable. He was an incredibly good-looking man. He was also a man in a precarious situation. She needed to lock that down. He was grateful to her right now. But emotions were always heightened in these kinds of situations. And she was well aware of it.

So she shoved those feelings away and focused on the mission at hand: getting the Ortizes to safety.

And hopefully today they would be well on their way to doing that.

CHAPTER FORTY-NINE

RAFE

"SOFIA, you need to put on some clothes."

Sofia stomped her foot, crossing her arms over her chest. "I *like* these pajamas," she said with a stubborn set to her jaw.

Rafe sighed as he ran a hand through his hair. He had not gotten enough sleep to deal with this. It was going to be a rough day, and he just wanted Sofia and Enzo to be fully dressed. The handler was supposed to come by in about two hours, and he wanted to check off getting the kids dressed so that he could focus.

But once again, his children had decided they had other plans.

He looked around the room, blowing out a breath and praying for patience. "You know what? Fine. Stay in your pajamas. But after breakfast, you have to get changed."

Sofia nodded, her stubbornness disappearing as she gave him a sweet smile. "Of course, Papa."

She skipped past him and out of the room.

Rafe needed a nap. At times like this, he felt like he was getting whiplash from how quickly his kids' moods changed. He couldn't shift gears quite as fast, however. And he still felt a lingering resentment at the fact that she had put up such a fight about the pajamas to begin with.

He blew out another breath and looked over at Enzo, who stared at him with big eyes. "I guess you want to stay in your pajamas for a little while too?"

Enzo nodded slowly at him.

"Okay, fine. Let's go get some breakfast, and everybody can get changed after."

Enzo ran over to him and hugged him.

Rafe felt some of his annoyance slip away. He rested his hand on the back of Enzo's head. "I love you too, buddy."

He picked up Enzo and carried him down the stairs.

Outside the room, he looked for Sofia, but he didn't see her. He turned for the stairs. When he reached the bottom, he heard her chattering away. He followed the sound of her voice to the kitchen. She was carrying on an animated conversation with Bishop.

Nola stood over by the stove flipping pancakes. He stopped at the sight of her. Yesterday he'd had trouble imagining her as a mom. Right now she stood in her bare feet with her hair pulled back in a messy bun, flipping pancakes and stirring scrambled eggs.

"Hey, Rafe. Morning," Bishop called.

"Morning," Rafe said, his gaze on Nola.

She looked over her shoulder at him. "Pancakes are just about ready."

Bishop slid off her stool and went to go grab the plates from the cabinet before placing them on the counter. Nola grabbed the frying pan of scrambled eggs and placed it on the counter on a thick mat.

After flipping three more pancakes from the pan, she placed them on the already tall stack and brought them to the counter, placing them next to the bacon that was already there. An assortment of cut fruit on a separate platter completed the breakfast display.

Rafe smiled at the spread. "I was just hoping we would be able to find some cold cereal."

"It's a big day. We should have a big breakfast," Ileana said as she sailed into the room. She was once again perfectly coiffed, as if she had been up and ready for hours. She walked over to the coffee pot and held it up. "Coffee?"

"I would love some," he said.

Nola leaned back against the counter, her own coffee mug nestled in her hands. "Go ahead and grab some food while it's hot."

Rafe made plates for the kids, placed them on the table, and then went back for his own.

Nola stepped next to him. "How'd you sleep?"

He glanced over his shoulder at the kids, but Bishop was keeping them entertained. "Not great."

"Understandable. Ileana's contacted a lawyer for you. Her name's Chandra Wilson. She is very, very good. She'll be here in about an hour to discuss your case with you before the handler arrives."

Rafe's concern about someone else being brought in must have shown on his face.

"You don't have to worry about Chandra. Ileana and I both worked with her for years in the intelligence field. She switched over to run her own national security law firm five years ago. She is the lawyer people *want* on their side."

Once again, he was bowled over by how above and beyond Nola and her mother-in-law had gone for them. "Thank you."

Nola brushed off the thanks without comment. "But no matter how it goes today, Ileana and I have been talking about some plans. We'll find a way to make sure that you and your family are safe."

Rafe looked into her eyes and knew she meant it. "Thank you," he said again.

This time, she gave him a small smile. "Of course."

She took her plate and headed over to the table. Rafe loaded up a plate for himself, suddenly feeling hungry. And he knew it was because a burden had been lifted. He was still the one in charge of his family's safety, but he was no longer the only one looking out for them.

CHAPTER FIFTY

NOLA

AFTER BREAKFAST, Nola went upstairs to get changed. When she returned, only Avad was in the kitchen, tidying up from breakfast and pulling together a tray. Nola looked around, surprised that Ileana wasn't there.

Avad read her look. "She's in her office. Chandra just arrived. She said you should go and join them as soon as you came down."

Then Avad picked up a coffee pot and placed it on a tray that he'd already arranged with cups and saucers. He started to pick it up, but Nola waved him off. "I'll take it."

Nodding his thanks, Avad turned his attention back to the ingredients he'd laid out on the counter. "Good. I thought I would make some cupcakes for Mol— Sofia and Enzo."

Nola's heart twisted a little at the slipup. Avad always used to have some sweet treat ready for Molly when she was here. And just at this moment, she realized how much he must have missed being able to do that. "I'm sure they'd love that."

She lifted the tray and turned down the second hallway that branched off the main hallway. Ileana's bedroom was down there as well as her office. She'd move down here when her husband had died, not wanting to sleep in the room that they had shared for nearly forty years.

The door to the office was ajar slightly. Nola nudged it open with her foot. "Knock, knock."

Ileana smiled from her spot on the couch. "Oh, there you are. Good. I see Avad told you Chandra is here."

Nola placed the tray on the table in front of Ileana. Chandra stood up from the couch next to her.

Chandra was tall at five foot eleven. African American with a close-cut hairstyle, she always reminded Nola of a high-fashion model. Today she was no less fashionable in a fuchsia suit that showed off her long muscular legs.

More than one poor fool had underestimated Chandra based on her good looks. She was formidable in the courtroom and perhaps equally as formidable in the field. Back in her intelligence days, she and Nola had ended up in some dicey situations. The woman could handle herself.

Nola extended her hand. "Good to see you, Chandra."

Chandra returned the shake, a warm smile on her face. "You too, Nola. It's been too long."

Nola didn't respond to that statement, knowing that Chandra was saying it one, because she meant it, and two, because it was customary. Chandra was well aware of why Nola hadn't been around.

Nola took a seat across from them.

Chandra retook her seat, crossing her long legs at the ankles. She eyed Nola. "You look good. From the way Ileana talked, I expected you to be one step removed from a cavewoman."

Nola grinned. "Only in manners."

Chandra chuckled. "Oh, so nothing's changed, then."

Nola smiled, and then it faded from her face as she spoke. "So I take it Ileana has brought you up to speed?"

Chandra nodded, her face becoming all business as well. "Yes. The US Attorney's office has changed since you were last a part of it. They'll try and squeeze Mr. Ortiz for every ounce of information without providing him with anything in return. Budgets are tight. There's not a lot of money for witness protection anymore. Most of the money previously earmarked for protection is going to other critical efforts." Chandra rolled her eyes, giving a clear opinion of what she thought of those particular efforts.

"So what do you suggest?" Ileana asked.

Chandra smiled. "I suggest what I always suggest to my clients: they stay quiet and let me do all the talking."

CHAPTER FIFTY-ONE

RAFE

RAFE WALKED down the stairs as nervous butterflies zoomed through his stomach. The US attorney would be here soon. His own attorney had already arrived, but he had yet to meet her. He'd been busy getting Sofia and Enzo situated. Bishop was curled up with them now in the den upstairs, watching a movie.

But Sofia hadn't wanted her father to leave right away. It had taken more than a little coaxing to get her to let him go, even though he assured her he would be downstairs. He knew this was only the beginning. That clinginess was going to get worse. He'd have to find someone who could help them. But first he needed to make sure all of them were safe.

Avad walked next to him quietly. As they reached the bottom of the stairs, he motioned toward a hallway that Rafe had not been down before.

"Chandra is a good lawyer. More than that, she's a good person. She'll do right by you," Avad said.

Rafe was too nervous to do much more than nod his head in understanding. They approached an open door. Rafe could hear feminine voices inside.

Avad knocked on the door and pushed it open. Three sets of eyes turned to him. Rafe immediately felt better at seeing Ileana and Nola, but the new woman gave him pause. Stunning and well put together, she assessed him just as coolly as he assessed her. She stood, extending her hand. "Mr. Ortiz, I'm Chandra Wilson."

Rafe reached out and shook her hand. She had a strong grip, a no-nonsense grip. Rafe was a believer in a handshake telling you a great deal about a person. In Chandra's case, it told him that she was a straight shooter and confident. It eased his worry a little, but only a little.

Ileana stood and gestured to the chair next to Nola. "Can I get you some coffee, Rafe?"

Rafe shook his head. He was nervous enough. The last thing he needed was more caffeine. "No, thank you."

Ileana nodded, retaking her seat. Rafe slid into his seat, shooting a look at Nola. She met his gaze and gave him a slight nod.

Chandra leaned forward. "First, I want to say how sorry I am for all that you and your family have been through. I also have to tell you how impressed I am at how you have survived these last few days. It's a testament to your commitment to your family."

"And to Nola's protective abilities," Rafe added.

Chandra shot a grin at Nola. "Oh, I'm well aware of those. And I know you don't know me well enough to trust me, but Ileana and Nola do. So I need to ask you to trust me when the US DA arrives. You cannot say *anything* unless I give you the okay. And to be perfectly honest, I don't think I'm going to be giving the okay at all. I would prefer if you weren't even in the room for this meeting. But I understand from Ileana that you want to be there."

Ileana had talked to him about that earlier, but Rafe needed to hear what was said. He wasn't at full trust yet with anyone, not when it came to his family's safety. He nodded.

"I understand that," Chandra said. "But I do still request that you say nothing unless I give you the go-ahead."

Rafe nodded. "I have no problem with that."

Chandra grinned again. "Excellent."

They spent the next few minutes going over some details of the case with Chandra explaining what she wanted to do. Rafe answered the questions fully, knowing that at this point, he had nothing to lose.

Nola's phone beeped, and she glanced down at it. "It's Avad. The US Attorney just pulled up."

Chandra took a sip of her coffee and then wiped her lips. "Okay, Mr. Ortiz, you say nothing. Not a single word. You don't even breathe loudly without my permission, is that clear?"

Rafe nodded.

"No matter what I say, you stay there silent and without any expression on your face. Can you handle that?"

Sit stiff and without expression, that he could do. He nodded.

"Good."

They sat in silence for the next two minutes before heavy footsteps sounded down the hall. There was a knock at the door, and then Avad stepped in and aside to allow US District Attorney Brent Ackers access.

Rafe tensed. *Here we go.*

CHAPTER FIFTY-TWO

NOLA

US ATTORNEY ACKERS stepped into the room and paused. His gaze roved over everyone there. He was in his early fifties, with hair that was just starting to gray along the crown. He had a surprisingly decent tan for a man who hadn't been on a vacation in a year. He probably went to a tanning booth.

Nola had done a background check on Ackers. As a US marshal, he'd been injured in the line of duty, so he went back to law school, and that was how he'd ended up there. He'd been with his current department for the last ten years and had a good record. He hadn't lost anyone.

Nola noted he wore an expensive suit but not a brand-new one. His shoes, however, did have a high shine to them. His gaze fastened on Ileana. He smiled. "Director Hamilton, it's a pleasure to finally meet you."

Ileana stood, inclining her head. "And you as well, Mr. Ackers. Would you please take a seat?" She indicated the seat next to her. It was the least comfortable chair in the room.

Nola bit back a smile at that. Ileana wanted Ackers to know where he stood in the pecking order.

As his gaze found the chair, his mask of civility slipped for a moment. And Nola knew he understood what Ileana was doing. He nodded his head. "Thank you."

He moved around to his chair, and Chandra stepped forward. "I'm Chandra Wilson."

Ackers's eyebrows rose at her introduction. He put out his hand. "I didn't realize you would be here."

Chandra smiled back at him. "I was recently hired as Mr. Ortiz's attorney."

Ackers's eyebrows nearly completely disappeared into his hairline at that announcement. He shot a glance at Rafe, suspicion clouding his features. He'd expected Rafe to be here alone or only with Ileana. Chandra's presence hadn't been considered and had thrown Ackers.

Nola wasn't sure if that was good or bad.

A short time later, she was sure it was good for them and bad for Ackers. Ackers had spent the last five minutes explaining what Ortiz was going to have to do in order to get the United States government's protection. He made it sound as if they were doing him a huge favor and were getting absolutely nothing out of the deal.

Ackers's chest puffed out as he continued to speak, his confidence growing. "So as you can see, it is quite a burden on the United States government—"

Finally Chandra had had enough. She cut him off. "Oh, please. You have been looking for the ones responsible for Agent Bowers's death for two years now. You have also been looking for a way to take down the cartel and their resources in the United States for even longer. Mr. Ortiz offers you both. So please stop with all this nonsense about how the United States government is doing the Ortiz family a favor. The United States government doesn't do favors."

Ackers's mouth shifted to a tight line. "Yes, well, of course the United States does have *some* vested interest in this case. However, we cannot just guarantee protection to anyone, even if there is a great deal of risk against them. Why, then just anyone could ask for protection."

Nola gripped the side of her chair to keep from hitting the man.

Chandra, however, appeared completely unruffled. "Yes, but not everyone has the information that Mr. Ortiz does."

Ackers inclined his head. "Speaking of which, I will need to verify the information before any deal can be made. So if Mr. Ortiz were to hand over the evidence he has—"

Chandra cut him off again. "Absolutely not." She stood up. "This meeting is not going anywhere. If you are unwilling to provide Mr. Ortiz with what he needs, we'll find someone who can. So I think we can bring this meeting to a—"

This time it was Ackers who cut in. "I didn't say that. I merely suggested that there would be a more efficient way to make this happen. Being Mr. Ortiz is already here, and you as well, perhaps we could get the deposition out of the way."

Chandra smiled at him again. "He's not saying a word until we have everything ironed out in an agreement. As soon as he fulfills his part of the agreement, you will protect him and his family. Otherwise, he's not saying a word."

"We need to—" Ackers spluttered.

Chandra leaned forward. "Not. A. Word."

Ackers sat back and then turned to Ileana. "Mrs. Hamilton,

of course you understand that there are more concerns here than simply the safety of the Ortiz family."

"I completely agree with Ms. Wilson. Perhaps you are not the district attorney we need to speak with. I'm sure someone else would like to help out the Ortiz family, which of course would help out their career greatly."

Ackers nearly fell out of his chair in his haste to respond. "I didn't say I didn't want to help. I just need to make some arrangements."

Chandra narrowed her eyes. "We are prepared to provide a deposition first thing tomorrow morning. You will need to send over the contract to my office no later than this afternoon guaranteeing the Ortiz family witness protection for the rest of their lives."

Ackers hedged. "It will take my office some time to get such a contract together."

"Oh, you don't have to worry about that. I've already drafted one. I can send it over to your office immediately."

Ackers's voice was now stiff. "That would be very helpful."

"Well, I believe we have an understanding." Chandra stood.

Ackers got to his feet more slowly, looking a little bewildered. Nola almost felt bad for the guy.

Almost.

Ileana, however, seemed to take pity on the poor fella. "Mr. Ackers, why don't I walk you out?"

"Um, yes, uh, thank you," Ackers said, following Ileana from the room.

Chandra took her seat with a grin. "That was fun."

Rafe looked even more bewildered than Ackers. "Was that good?"

Chandra nodded. "That was very good. If all goes well, and they accept the contract as-is, with a few minor changes, you will be providing your deposition early tomorrow morning, and then you will be in the custody and under the protection of the United States government immediately thereafter." Chandra smiled. "This is what you wanted, Mr. Ortiz, and it looks like you're going to get everything you want."

CHAPTER FIFTY-THREE

RAFE

LIGHT CAME from outside the windows. Rafe stared around the darkened room as he sat up in the bed, his arms protectively cradling Enzo and Sofia.

After Ackers had left, he sat with Chandra for hours, going over his testimony for tomorrow. Nola had slipped out of the room, giving the two of them their privacy. It had been a draining experience. Afterwards, he'd wanted to do nothing but sleep. In fact, he'd made his way back to the bedroom and lay down. When he'd awoken, both Enzo and Sofia were curled up asleep next to him.

They'd spent the rest of the day playing outside, helping Avad decorate cupcakes and just spending time with one another. When darkness fell, the kids had quickly drifted off to sleep. Rafe, however, once again had doubts and worries crowd into his mind. He'd finally fallen off to sleep when Sofia startled awake from a nightmare. It had been impossible to get her to go back to sleep right away. But after two hours, she had finally drifted off, her hands clutched tightly in his. But sleep still eluded him.

He'd meet with the US attorney later today and provide a deposition.

Rafe had known it would come to this. Ever since he'd first started gathering data, he'd known it would end up like this. And yet somehow he was struggling to believe that the moment was finally here.

And he was terrified. There was no going back now. When he first started down this road, he'd been a single man. He'd been completely focused on doing what was right. He knew what the correct line of action was. Now the stakes were so much higher. He'd already lost Mariana. And now he had Sofia and Enzo. He'd brought all this horror into their young lives.

At the same time, that horror would have been in their lives even if he had done nothing. Tijuana was not a safe place. It was almost impossible to escape the violence that racked the city unscathed. There was no guarantee if he had just kept his head down that Enzo and Sofia would've been safe. They could've grown up and gotten involved unintentionally with the cartel themselves. They could have been one of the dozens of innocent victims that had been killed just because they were in the wrong place at the wrong time.

He looked around the room. Now they were in America. And for now, they were safe.

But they wouldn't be if they stayed with him.

He knew that witness protection was the best call for him. It was truly his only hope. But he wanted more for Sofia and Enzo. He wanted them to have a real life. He wanted them to go to school, have friends, and not have to look over their shoulders all the time. And to be honest, he knew how deep the cartel's tentacles reached. And he had a feeling that the witness protection would only be a stop gag. Eventually the cartel would find him, especially when it came close to the trial. They would more than double their efforts to locate him.

He took a shaky breath, knowing what he had to do. He got up and stood, looking down at his kids. God, he loved them so much.

He headed to the shower, leaving the door open so that he could hear them as he turned on the water. He stripped off his clothes and stepped in. The water was cold, but that was what he wanted. He didn't want to linger. He washed quickly and then stepped back out.

The towel was around his waist as he glanced back out into the room. The kids were both still sleeping. Sofia had shifted over so that now she was curled up protectively around Enzo. He always found her like that in the morning.

He toweled off and slipped on his sweatpants and a clean T-shirt. Then he glanced at the clock. It was four thirty. The light wouldn't be up for at least another hour or two. He looked at the chair by the fireplace. It would probably be better if he sat there. But he found himself climbing back into the bed. He wasn't sure how much time he would have with them, and he wanted to spend every minute he could.

CHAPTER FIFTY-FOUR

NOLA

THE CLOCK FACE READ five as Nola opened her eyes. She wasn't surprised. Rising early was her hallmark. She stared up at the familiar ceiling, thinking about the events to come. Bishop had run a full background check on US Attorney Ackers. He was completely clean, bordering on dull.

He had no debt to speak of. No significant other in his life. He was one of the first in the office in the morning and one of the last out at night. He was, for all intents and purposes, married to the job. He would not be an easy mark for the cartel.

It was highly unlikely, but not impossible, that he was compromised. Bishop had run his phone records, and there were no red flags. There were no questionable numbers and no links between those numbers and either MS-13 or the cartel. He'd never lost one of his people. So it looked like everything was on the up and up.

And yet Nola was unsettled.

It was probably just that she had to put her faith in the government. They had brutally demonstrated that that faith was not always well-placed.

Pushing back the blankets, Nola sat on the edge of the bed. A nervous energy ran over her skin. A run would be good to lose some of the stress, but she didn't want to be away from the Ortizes this morning.

She didn't look too deeply at that thought and just accepted that it was what it was. Hefting herself from the bed, she headed for the shower. Hot water beat down on her, and she lowered her head. Chandra had contacted them last night after the contract had been signed. This morning, Nola was going to take Rafe to the US attorney to be deposed. Once the deposition was done, Avad would bring Sofia and Enzo, and they would be immediately placed into protective custody.

Today would be the last time she saw any of them.

Her chest ached at the thought. Somehow, in a very short time, the Ortiz family had snuck into her heart. But this was what was best for them. She turned off the shower and stepped out. After she toweled off, even though it was early, she put on her suit. The dark-navy coat was a little longer than most to allow her to hide her weapons, a holdover habit from her days at the CIA. She dried her hair enough so that it didn't soak her shirt and then left it.

A soft knock sounded at her bedroom door. She frowned, narrowing her eyes.

Ileana and Avad would have texted first if they needed something this early in the morning. Bishop would barge right in. Which meant it could only be one person. She quietly crossed the room and pulled open the door.

Rafe stood there. He had on a white T-shirt with suit pants, his feet bare. He gave her a small grimace. "Sorry. I know it's early, but I was hoping I could talk to you before the kids woke up."

Nola stepped back. "Come on in."

Rafe stepped inside and looked around the room. His gaze went to the picture of David and Molly that sat on the side table before it returned to her face. He took a breath then let it out slowly. "I have something to ask you."

She searched his face. Had he changed his mind? Was he not going to the deposition?

"I don't want the kids to go into protective custody with me."

Nola was floored by the statement and then realized she shouldn't have been. "You're worried about them being in the crosshairs."

"Yeah." He took a seat on the edge of the bed. "I know that that's what we agreed to, but with me, they're in danger. They won't have a chance at a normal life."

"They want to be with you."

Rafe ran a hand through his hair, causing it to stick straight up. "I know. And I want to be with them." His voice broke on the last word, then he cleared his throat. "But you know and I know that when the time for the trial comes, the cartel will pull out all the stops trying to find me. And they have a habit of finding the witnesses against them."

Nola couldn't disagree with that. "Don't you want to spend that time with your kids?"

"If something happens to me, they'll be devastated. But I'm hoping that by then, they will have found people who love them, who care about them. It will help them get through it."

Rafe believed he was going to die. And he wanted to make sure the kids had the right people around them to survive that. Her chest tightened as the image of Rafe being gunned down wafted through her mind. "It won't come to that, Rafe."

He gave her a smile. "You're an incredible woman, Nola. We

wouldn't be alive if it weren't for you. But not even you can give a guarantee like that." He took a breath. "Can you help find my kids a home? Somewhere that they'll be loved, where they can have a normal life?"

"Rafe, you don't have to decide this right now. There's so much else going on. Give yourself some time to—"

Rafe stood up from the bed. "No. This is how it has to be. I need to know they're safe. And right now, safe means they need to be away from me. Will you help me? Will you help them?"

Nola looked into his eyes. Everything in her being wanted to say no, that he was crazy, that everything would be fine, and that they would all be together. But she didn't believe in fairy tales either.

"Yes."

CHAPTER FIFTY-FIVE

BISHOP

BISHOP HAD HAD A LATE NIGHT. She'd done a deeper dive on the US attorney but had turned up nothing concerning. The guy was a Boy Scout. According to Nola, he was also complete tool, but he was on the up and up. There were no red flags when it came to him.

Yawning, Bishop made her way down the stairs. She wanted to grab a bite to eat and then hang out with the kids. She hoped she could distract them until their dad had to leave. She and Avad were going with Nola and Rafe to check the security and make sure everything and everybody was on the up and up. Then once the deposition was done she and Avad would return and bring the kids to Rafe.

Bishop didn't like that they didn't have a location yet. At the same time, she recognized that it was good that they weren't broadcasting where they would be. Still, a lot could go wrong.

But so far, she hadn't picked up any traces that the cartel knew that Rafe was coming in today. Of course, that didn't guarantee anything either.

The first floor was empty. She wandered down the hall to the kitchen. Only Ileana sat at the kitchen table. "Morning, my dear," she called.

Bishop stifled another yawn. "Morning," she mumbled as she headed for the coffee machine, clutching her robe around her. Ileana didn't say anything else, knowing that Bishop needed at least a few sips of coffee in the morning before she wanted to talk.

Bishop stood against the counter sipping her coffee, letting her mind go blank for a few moments. Finally, she roused herself and made her way over to the table.

Ileana placed a croissant and a jar of strawberry jam in front of Bishop as she sat down. Bishop took it with a nod of thanks and immediately cut the croissant and swiped some jam over it. "Where is everybody?"

"Rafe took the children down to the lake. Nola and Avad went with them."

Bishop glanced at the clock. "Everything still on schedule?"

"Yes. They'll be leaving in about thirty minutes."

Bishop took a bite and finished eating her croissant in silence while Ileana scanned the headlines on her tablet.

The back door opened, and Nola stepped in.

Bishop started at the sight of her. She was wearing one of her old suits. Bishop hadn't seen her in a suit in over two years. She smiled. "Nola, looking good."

Nola rolled her eyes, but Bishop caught the small smile playing around her lips. "When in Rome. I'm glad you're up. I need to speak with you two."

Bishop wiped the corner of her mouth with a napkin and placed it on the table. "What's up?"

"There's been a change of plans."

Nola explained how Rafe had come to speak with her and asked that the children not be placed in witness protection. Bishop's jaw dropped at the news. "Those poor kids."

"He's trying to do what he thinks is best for them. He's trying to keep them safe," Ileana said softly.

Nola nodded. "I tried to talk him out of it, but he wants them to have a normal life. And he doesn't think that they can do that with him. He doesn't think he has much of a life left."

Bishop started at the statement. Rafe was a nice man. He seemed like a really good father. And Bishop had seen him looking at Nola in a way that made Bishop a little hopeful.

"So I need to change things up a little bit," Nola said. "Bishop, I want you and Avad to follow us to the deposition."

Bishop frowned. "Follow you?"

"Rafe thinks that the cartel has tentacles everywhere. I have to admit I'm a little unsettled at the moment too. So I want you two to follow us and run facial recognition on anyone you see around us. Okay?"

"Okay," Bishop said.

Nola turned to Ileana. "I have something to ask you. It's kind of big, but can the children stay with you until we figure out their living arrangement?"

"Of course. I'm happy to have them here."

"Good."

"And if everything is on the up and up? And if Rafe is taken into protective custody today?" Bishop asked.

Nola sighed and looked out the window to where Rafe, Avad, and the kids had just come into view. "Then we do as Rafe wishes. We find a family that can give Sofia and Enzo a normal life."

CHAPTER FIFTY-SIX

NOLA

THE INSTRUCTIONS for where to meet Ackers had come in. Rafe was in the living room when she called him out into the hall to tell him. His face paled, and he gave her an abrupt nod. "When do we leave?"

"Ten minutes."

A small tremor ran through him, but he only nodded. Without another word, he turned on his heel and walked back into the living room where the kids were playing Candyland. Bishop looked up from where she was reading on the couch. Nola waved her over. She dropped her voice. "We're leaving in ten minutes. Can you find Ileana?"

Bishop looked back into the room where Rafe was moving toward the kids. Pain flashed across her eyes, and her chin trembled for a moment. "God, this sucks," she said before she hurried down the hall.

Nola pulled out her phone and texted Avad. *Ten minutes.* She slid her phone back in her pocket and stood at the living room door. She knew she should probably give the family some privacy, but she couldn't make herself step away.

Rafe was talking low, so Nola couldn't hear his words. But she saw the change run through the kids. The smiles they'd had on their faces slowly dimmed until they were gone. Enzo looked at his father and then looked down at the ground. But Sofia threw herself at her father. "No! No! You can't leave us!"

Tears pressed against the back of Nola's eyes at Sofia's outburst. Her chest tightened. But it wasn't Sofia and the torrent of emotion that pulled her focus.

It was Enzo.

He just looked resigned, his attention on his feet. And no five-year-old should be so used to life beating them down that they no longer reacted.

Nola forced herself away from the door. She took a few steps back into the hall and took a few deep breaths. She shouldn't have watched that. Their pain was too visceral. They were a family being destroyed in front of her eyes.

And she didn't need to see or feel that again.

She walked down the hall, stopping at Avad's office. He stood at his closet, collecting weapons and magazines. He turned when Nola stepped into the room. He nodded to a bag on the desk. "That's yours. There's a vest in there for Rafe as well."

Nola glanced in the bag. Avad did know how to pack a bag. She slipped off her suit jacket and pulled on the bulletproof vest. She pulled on the double holster and loaded it up and placed a Browning at her one hip and an FN 509 at her other. She grabbed the clips and placed them in her pockets.

Then she pulled her jacket back on and buttoned it up. The jacket had a high collar, so the vest wasn't noticeable. The rest of the gear she would have to leave in the bag. But Avad would be nearby with it. She slipped a couple of knives into the ridges on her boots then stood up and glanced at the hallway, not wanting to walk out there and realizing what a coward she was for it.

Avad snapped his bag closed. "He's a good man, Rafe. This is not an easy day for any of them."

And once again Nola felt that old anger bubble up at the fact that doing the right thing was going to destroy yet another family.

CHAPTER FIFTY-SEVEN

RAFE

RAFE FELT as if someone had reached into his chest, yanked out his heart, and then stomped on it in front of him. Sofia was inconsolable, sobbing in front of him. She had been so good these last couple of months, but now it seemed like everything had fallen on her at once. Rafe didn't know what to do or what to say to make it better. He didn't think there was anything he could.

Enzo was the complete opposite. He hadn't said a word. He'd barely moved a muscle. He just sat down and looked at the ground. He hadn't looked at his father since Rafe had said that he wouldn't be seeing them for a while.

He felt like a monster. And he was. Who walked away from their children like this?

Ileana slipped into the room. Rafe looked up at her, and she gave him a smile filled with compassion. "They're waiting for you outside."

Rafe took a shuddering breath. He leaned down and hugged Enzo to him. "I love you. Mama loves you too. Don't ever forget that."

There were so many other things he wanted to say. He wanted to tell Enzo how he was proud of him, that he was going to be an incredible man one day. He wanted to tell him that he should look after his sister and do the right things. But the words were clogged in his throat. So he just hugged his son tight and prayed that Enzo had a good life.

He turned to Sofia. She pushed him away. "No. No!"

"Sofia, Sofia, honey, I have to go."

"No! You can't leave us!"

He reached over and grabbed her, pulling her tight. She resisted at first and then collapsed in his arms, hugging him and sobbing as if her world was ending.

And he knew it was. He kissed her on the forehead as tears rolled down his cheeks. "I love you. I love you so much. Someday I hope you understand why I had to do this."

Sofia didn't respond. She just sobbed harder. He looked up at Ileana, feeling helpless. Ileana walked over and gently took Sofia from him. Sofia put up a small fight but then collapsed against Ileana.

Rafe leaned down and kissed Enzo on the forehead one more time and then walked out of the room. Every step was harder than the one before.

How could he do this? How could he?

But then he pictured Mariana as he'd last seen her. His resolve hardened as he wiped his cheeks. He could do this. Because it would allow them to live. Standing at the front door, his hand trembled on the knob. He leaned his head against the door. *God give me strength.*

Then he opened the door and walked out to his new life.

CHAPTER FIFTY-EIGHT

NOLA

WHEN THE DOOR opened and Rafe stepped through, Nola had to look away. The pain on his face was too much to bear.

Avad and Bishop sat in a Jaguar SUV on the other side of the roundabout. When Rafe appeared, Avad put the car in gear and pulled away.

Rafe walked over to her, looking like a man about to bolt. But he squared his shoulders and met her gaze across the roof of the car. He gave her a nod. "Let's go."

He opened the passenger door and pulled the bulletproof vest off the seat. Shrugging off his jacket, he pulled the vest on and then took a seat, his jacket in his lap.

Nola glanced over her shoulder at the house and then climbed into the driver's seat. Without a word, she put the car in gear, and they headed down the drive.

Rafe let out a trembling breath as they left Ileana's property.

His head was turned to the window, his fists clenched tightly in his lap. He was barely holding it together. She kept quiet, letting him work through everything in his mind.

The drive took thirty minutes. And for the first twenty-five, Rafe didn't say a word. Nola didn't push him to speak. She knew how gut-wrenching today was for him. If she'd had to step away from Molly . . .

She couldn't imagine it. Even in death, she'd been unable to let Molly go.

Rafe cleared his throat. "How much farther?"

"About five minutes. We're heading to a law office. It's a small firm, only two partners. They agreed to let us use the conference room. It was set up this morning, last minute, so no one should know that we're here."

Rafe nodded, his gaze straight ahead. "You'll look in on them from time to time, right?"

"Yes. I'll make sure they're safe. I'll make sure they're happy."

"Thank you. For everything."

For once, Nola wasn't comfortable in the silence. She didn't know what to say. The air was thick with emotion. She hoped that Rafe would be able to pull it all back so that he could focus on the deposition. At the same time, she wondered if that was even possible.

In the distance, Nola noticed the law building they were heading to. It was a home that had been converted into offices. All the homes on the street had been converted into businesses. The legal office was on the corner with a florist on one side and a bakery on the other. An optometrist was across the street.

Nola nodded toward the building. "That's where we're headed." She tapped her earbud. "Guys? Everything good?"

"All good. He hasn't arrived yet. But Chandra's here."

"I've got cameras covering the front and the back. Oh, wait.

Car's pulling in now." Bishop paused. "Looks like it's our guy. We're a go."

"Roger."

Nola turned to Rafe. "Ackers just arrived. Are you ready?"

Rafe ran a hand over his face as if wiping away the emotions of the morning. Finally, he nodded. "Yes. Let's get this over with."

CHAPTER FIFTY-NINE

BISHOP

THERE WERE ONLY two other cars in the parking lot where Avad and Bishop sat. Bishop had her laptop on her lap as she scrolled through the different images of the building. Avad had already done a walkthrough of the building itself. The lawyers who owned the building would not be in until after the deposition was concluded. They had given the keys to the building to the US attorney. So it would only be Nola, Rafe, Chandra, Ackers, and two US marshals.

Next to her, Avad picked up the camera and aimed it at the car. The US attorney stepped out. Avad took a shot of Ackers's face. Immediately, he appeared on Bishop's screen. She ran the facial recognition program, even though she knew who it was, and it immediately came back with a positive. "That's him."

Chandra shook his hand. The two moved up to the porch.

A Buick SUV pulled in next to Ackers's car. Bishop stared at the car, waiting for the men to appear.

The driver stepped out. He was a tall man with dark hair and pale skin. He wore a gray suit a little too small for him. "Looks like you put on some weight there, Marshal."

His partner was shorter and stockier. He was blond with a tanned complexion. Avad snapped shots of both of them, and once again the images appeared on Bishop's laptop. She quickly ran them through the facial recognition program and frowned when the match didn't come back automatically.

Avad glanced over at her. "Problem?"

Bishop didn't answer right away, staring at the screen. Finally, the screen blinked green. "No, we're good."

She stared at the images. The taller one was Charles Graham. And the blond one was Neil Blanco.

She tapped the mic at her throat. "Nola, we have confirmation. You're good to go."

A few seconds later, Nola's car pulled into the parking lot. Nola stepped out of the driver's door, casting a glance around. Bishop smiled. Classic Nola. Someone could tell her that things were safe, but she would still have her guard up.

Finally, Nola leaned down and said something. Rafe appeared from the passenger seat.

Bishop sucked in a breath at the sight of him. Poor guy, he looked devastated. She understood what he was doing with his kids. She also knew how much it was killing him. It was written all over his face.

Nola cast another glance around the parking lot, stopping her gaze for a second on the car with Avad and Bishop before she turned and escorted Rafe inside.

Bishop closed her laptop.

"Looks like it's about to begin," Avad said.

Bishop nodded, glancing down at her laptop. The recognition

had taken longer than it should have. It was possible it was just a slow internet connection, although that shouldn't have been a problem. She hesitated for just a second and then flipped open the laptop.

"Problem?" Avad asked.

"Probably not. I just want to check something."

CHAPTER SIXTY

NOLA

THE LAW OFFICES of Schwab and Franklin were pretty bland. The carpet in the lobby was beige, as were the walls. Brown wooden chairs lined the walls of the small lobby. Across from the front of the door was a large desk with the Schwab and Franklin logo on the wall behind it. The desk was unmanned.

Nola stepped inside, casting a glance around. She'd gotten the layout of the building ahead of time. The lobby emptied into a hallway that had two offices on the right-hand side and two conference rooms on the left. At the back was a kitchen area that had also been set up as a lounge. The stairs were off the kitchen and led up to another few rooms that were only being used as storage.

Avad had done a run-through this morning and installed cameras. No one had been here since Avad. He said that everything looked on the up and up. She trusted Avad. But she still didn't let down her guard.

Chandra stepped into the lobby from the hallway. She smiled at Rafe. "You ready, Mr. Ortiz?"

Rafe gave her a stiff nod. "I think so."

"This way." Chandra started back down the hall.

Nola walked down the hall behind Rafe, casting a glance into the office on the right and then down the hall. No noise or movement came from them. Outside the conference room, one of the agents stood with Ackers.

When Chandra and Rafe reached them, Ackers nodded. "Rafael Ortiz, this is US Marshal Charles Graham. He will be handling your case after the deposition today."

The marshal extended his hand. "Mr. Ortiz."

Nola the studied the man, noticing that his suit was a little too tight. She walked past him without introduction following Rafe and the attorney into the conference room.

The blond second marshal was standing next to a long table. A laptop had been set up in front of it, along with a legal pad and a small recording device next to it. Ackers nodded to the other man. "This is Marshal Neil Blanco."

The marshal gave them a nod.

Ackers didn't introduce Nola, and the marshal raised an eyebrow at her. "And you are?"

"Here to make sure that Mr. Ortiz is safe until he's officially in your custody."

The man gave her a hard look and finally nodded. "Do you have a name?"

Nola stood against the wall. "I do." She crossed her arms over her chest. A small smile slipped across Chandra's face.

Ackers waved to the table. "Why doesn't everybody take a seat?"

Nola settled in against the wall as Chandra escorted Rafe

around the table. She nodded to him and whispered something in his ear.

The attorney picked up the recorder. "I'm going to record this deposition."

Chandra placed her own recorder on the table as well. "No problem."

Nola leaned back and settled in against the wall for the long wait.

CHAPTER SIXTY-ONE

BISHOP

BISHOP HUNCHED OVER HER COMPUTER. It had been an hour since Rafe, Chandra, and Nola had gone inside. Nola had kept her mic on so that Avad and Bishop could hear everything that was going on. Rafe provided detail after detail of the cartel's activities. Each one was more gruesome than the last.

Bishop, of course, knew about the cartel and their activities, but hearing Rafe speak about it just brought it to light in a whole new horrible way.

"And do you have any documentation that backs up these claims?" Ackers asked.

Rafe responded. "Yes. A flash drive that is filled with information as well as a drop box that I used for the physical contents."

"May I have the flash drive?" Ackers asked.

Rafe didn't respond. He didn't get a chance. Chandra cut in before Rafe could respond. "As soon as he hands the drive over, we consider his deal with the government complete. We will continue the deposition, but he will officially be under the US government's protection from that point forward. Do you agree?"

The US attorney hedged. "Well, if the flash drive proves to be—"

Chandra cut him off. "That is not what we agreed to. Either you agree that he is immediately put into witness protection, or this is where this meeting ends."

The attorney was quiet for a second before he grudgingly said, "Yes. As soon as he hands over the flash drive, that portion of the contract is initiated."

Go Chandra, Bishop thought, her gaze still on her screen.

She'd been searching the database, trying to see why there had been that pause when she'd searched for the marshals. It was probably nothing. Just a slow connection like she thought, but being it was the cartel they were watching for, she wanted to make sure. She'd shifted from the government database, however, because everything there had checked out.

On a hunch, she ran a simple Google search of each of the agents. The first hit she pulled up showed a tall man with dark hair who was extremely skinny. He really had put on weight. She zoomed in on his face and sucked in a breath. "Oh, no, no, no, no, no, no, no."

"What's wrong?" Avad asked.

Bishop didn't answer. She quickly initiated a second search, which brought up another newspaper clipping of the other marshal. She pulled up the shot from the database and compared the two images.

Her heart lodged in her throat. They didn't match.

Over the earpiece, she could hear Rafe. *"This is the flash drive. It has all the information that I have explained thus far and some additional information on some other cases."*

Bishop hit the mic at her throat. "Nola, the marshals are fake."

CHAPTER SIXTY-TWO

NOLA

THE DETAILS that Rafe had provided the attorney were gruesome. The stuff of nightmares. At the same time, Nola was amazed at how much information he'd been able to collect without the cartel being aware. It was truly astounding.

She watched Ackers taking the deposition, but nothing about him seemed off. He was still an arrogant jerk, but he was on the up and up.

The marshal sitting next to him, however, was a little concerning. He varied between looking bored and annoyed.

Experienced marshals knew that a large portion of their job was boring. But they all tended to have the same blasé look on their face. This agent didn't. He seemed bothered that he had to spend so much time listening to this.

Nola's Spidey sense tingled. But she had nothing concrete to base it on. Just a feeling that something wasn't right.

Of course, she'd stayed alive by listening to that sense. Nola shifted along the back of the room, making it look as if she was just stretching her legs after standing still for too long in one spot.

She walked to the other side of the room until she was to the marshal's left and slightly out of his vision. He'd have to turn to see her.

Ackers mentioned the flash drive, and all of a sudden the marshal tensed. Nola narrowed her eyes, unbuttoning her bottom suit jacket button so she had quicker access to her gun. But she acted as if she was going to put her hand in her pocket. She slipped her hand underneath her jacket and placed her hand on the butt of her gun.

The marshal didn't even notice. His attention was laser-focused on Rafe.

Nola watched as Rafe pulled the flash drive from his pocket. He'd carried it from Mexico, all the way through the last couple of months. He'd kept it on him at all times, even when sleeping.

Nola had noticed it the first night, but she said nothing to him about it. But now she could tell that the marshal was awfully interested in it.

It was entirely possible that he just had a history with the cartel and that he was personally involved in making sure that they were brought to justice. But Nola couldn't help but think that there was something else at play here.

Bishop's voice burst out across her earpiece. "Nola, the marshals are fake."

But Nola already had her weapon clear of the holster. The marshal pulled his own weapon, aiming it at Rafe. Nola shot first, the bullet catching the man in the shoulder.

"Get down!" Nola yelled.

Rafe and Chandra hit the deck, but the US attorney hesitated.

The second marshal burst into the room, his weapon pulled

as well. He let off a series of shots. Nola dove for the ground and shot from the floor, catching the man in the chest. His eyes closed, and he dropped.

Nola kicked the guns away from both marshals. She turned to the US attorney. A bullet had entered Ackers's back. He was slumped forward over the table, blood staining the back of his jacket. "Damn it."

"Nola, we have three cars heading for us. They're moving fast," Bishop said.

Chandra climbed out from underneath the table, and Nola tried to haul Ackers up. Chandra hurried over. "I've got him. Get Rafe out of here."

"No." Rafe took Ackers and hiked him over his shoulder in a fireman carry. Nola led the way to the door.

Rafe was right behind her.

They hurried out into the lobby and burst out the front door.

Avad and Bishop had moved the car so it was now at the front of the lot.

Rafe hurried to Chandra's car and dumped Ackers in the backseat. Nola leaped into the driver's seat of the Mercedes, put the key in the ignition, and threw it into reverse. She came to a screeching halt next to Rafe. "Get in!"

Rafe leapt into the passenger side.

Nola met Chandra's gaze, who gave her a nod before throwing her car into reverse and taking off for the rear entrance of the parking lot.

Nola put the car into drive and sped out of the lot. Avad and Bishop were right behind them. Three cars raced down the street toward them. Nola took a left, jamming on the gas. She flicked a gaze in the rearview mirror. One of the cars turned into the law office's parking lot; the other two stayed on the road, following them.

Damn it.

In Nola's mind, she pulled up the map of the area that she'd memorized last night. She and Avad had prepared for this.

Avad turned to the right, disappearing from Nola's rearview mirror.

Rafe glanced through the back window. "Where are they going?"

"It's okay. This is part of the plan."

Rafe glanced at her and then nodded. He reached for the glove compartment and pulled the gun case from inside.

"You ready?" Nola asked.

Rafe nodded. "Yeah."

"Good, then hang on."

She yanked the wheel to the right and tore down a side road. It was a busy street and people were already out. She wove through the traffic. A couple of cars of honked at her in annoyance but then quickly got out of the way when they saw the cars bearing down on them.

Nola prayed that nobody darted out into traffic and got hit. She didn't think the guys behind them would care too much about collateral damage.

She yanked the wheel to the left, entering a Home Depot parking lot with a squeal of tires.

The chase cars followed right behind her. One of them separated so that they were now racing parallel toward Nola and Rafe. The passenger windows of each car were rolled down. A man leaned out, spraying the back of Nola's car with gunfire. Rafe ducked, but none of the bullets made it into the car. The back window was now dotted with hits.

Rafe glanced back and then looked at Nola. "Bulletproof?"

Nola nodded. "Not my first rodeo."

Rafe gave her a small smile at that statement.

Nola sped forward, cutting around the Home Depot and speeding toward the back of the parking lot. A few shoppers were already out and had stopped to gawk at the car chase. They quickly ducked for cover when gunfire rang out.

Nola burst out of the parking lot quickly and pulled the wheel to the right. She barely missed side-swiping a minivan that screeched to a halt. But she didn't slow. She pressed down on the accelerator again, heading for the business park straight ahead.

Come on, Avad. Be ready. She tapped on her mic. "Almost there."

"In position," Avad said.

Nola smiled.

Rafe looked at her in disbelief. "Are you having fun?"

She shrugged. "A little bit."

Rafe shook his head as more gunfire peppered the back of the car. Nola pressed down as hard as she could on the accelerator, but that was about as fast as the car could go. She raced forward, going airborne for a moment as they sped over the entrance of the business park.

The business park was still under construction. The closest buildings were just shells with incomplete interiors. Nola counted as she slipped past buildings. One, two, three, four, five.

She yanked the wheel to the left.

Rafe let out a small grunt as he was slammed into the door.

Nola sped forward, spying the large warehouse at the back of the business park. The warehouse was only two stories high. The front garage door was open. Nola aimed for it. Up on the roof, two figures appeared.

Rafe leaned forward, staring at them. "Is that Avad and Bishop?"

"Yup."

"Are they holding—"

A rocket-propelled grenade soared over them and crashed into the car behind him. The car flipped and then crashed onto its side, sliding along the ground.

The second RPG hit the other car. It flipped over and landed on its hood. Nola eased off the accelerator so they rolled into the warehouse. She stopped and then put the car into reverse.

She raced in reverse back to the first car and slammed to a stop. She was out the door as soon as the car stopped, her gun in her hand.

She peered inside. One of the guys was gone. His face was no longer recognizable as human. The two guys who had been in the back had been ejected from the car. The passenger was still alive. Nola pulled him out from under from the window. She didn't have handcuffs.

What's a girl to do?

She slammed the butt of her gun into the back of his skull, and his eyes rolled back in his head.

She strode over to the other car. Her attention on the man in the street, she didn't notice the other one aiming over the car until it was too late. She whirled, knowing she wasn't going to be able to make the shot in time.

Gunshots cut through the air. The man at the car went flying back. She glanced over her shoulder.

Rafe gave her a nod. Nola turned back to the man in the street. He was gone. She inspected the other three members of the car, but they were all gone as well. One was still alive from the other car, though. Ackers could hopefully turn him and get as much information from him is possible.

If the attorney was still alive.

She tapped the mic at her throat. "Contact Chandra. See if she and the attorney are all right."

Taking in the devastation around him, Rafe walked up next to her. "You planned all this."

Nola shrugged. "I'm not very trusting."

"I think that's probably a very good thing." His mouth

dropped. "The flash drive. It's back at the office. The cartel's there."

Nola cut him off. "You don't have to worry about that. That was also part of the plan. Now they think they have all your info."

Rafe stared her. "What? But that was the only copy."

"That first night at Darrin's while you were asleep, I made a copy of the flash drive. I sent it to Bishop. Just as a little extra precaution."

He stared at her in shock, and then a smile crossed his face. "You had all the evidence all this time?"

Nola shrugged. "Yeah, sorry. But I needed you to sell it. I know what it cost you to get that evidence together. If anything happened to you or me, I wanted to make sure that the evidence still got out."

The smile dimmed from Rafe's face. "What do we do now?"

Nola smiled. "I have an idea about that too."

CHAPTER SIXTY-THREE

NOLA

AFTER THE SHOOT-OUT, Nola squired Rafe away. Avad and Bishop stayed with them, which left Chandra to handle the police. The US attorney had immediately gone into surgery. He was in for a long recovery, but the prognosis was good.

Against Rafe's objections, they headed back to Ileana's estate. Rafe didn't want to go back. Nola knew he didn't think he'd be able to leave Sofia and Enzo again. But Nola was counting on that no longer being necessary. She stopped at the estate only long enough to drop off Rafe and to see the happy reunion.

Then she and Avad left to initiate part two of their plan. It went like clockwork.

Now she sat on the back patio of Ileana's estate, watching the kids play with Rafe.

Sofia and Enzo had been so excited to see him they had been unwilling to let him out of their sight since his return.

Nola knew that if faced with the choice of leaving them behind again, Rafe wouldn't be able to do it. They were a family unit. They would continue on together.

Ileana stepped outside and sat down next to Nola.

Nola glanced over at her mother-in-law. "Well?"

"I had to pull a few strings, but it's done."

Nola searched her face. "Are you sure about this? It could be dangerous."

Ileana let out a laugh. "You're not the only one who can handle themselves, Nola. There will be danger for this family wherever they are. They might as well be somewhere where the kids are comfortable."

"Thank you for this. It's a really good thing you're doing."

"That *we* are doing," Ileana said.

Nola nodded.

Ileana indicated the family. "I think you should be the one to tell them."

"Oh, I don't think—"

"You should be the one to tell them." Ileana stood up and walked back inside the house.

Nola watched her go with a smile. Everyone thought that Nola was the stubborn one, but Ileana had her beat by miles. Nola didn't think the woman had ever been talked out of doing something that she intended to do.

Nola stood up and walked toward the family, her hands in her pockets. Enzo looked over at her as if trying to gauge what was coming. She gave him a smile. He smiled back and then continued gathering pinecones. She wasn't sure what exactly he intended to do with all of them.

Rafe looked up, the smile dimming on his face as it had on his son's. He also searched Nola's face, looking for a clue as to what she was bringing. She gave him a smile as well. Rafe said something to Sofia, who also looked over at Nola. The whole family was nervous. Hopefully this news would be the first step in changing that.

Rafe walked over to her and stopped when he was only a few inches in front of her. "What is it? What happened?"

"Nothing bad," she assured him. "In fact, if you agree to it, it could be something very good."

Nola indicated that they should step a little farther away from the kids. Rafe glanced over his shoulder at them and then followed her. He stopped when he was only a few inches away.

Nola had to crane her neck to look up at him. "I have good news and bad news for you. What would you like first?"

"I'll take the bad."

Nola smiled. She would have chosen the same way. "I'm afraid that Rafael Ortiz passed away this morning at 10:02 a.m. He succumbed to the gunshot wound he received while trying to avoid the cartel hit squad that was sent out after him."

He stared at her. "What?"

"At least, that's what the gunman who was taken to the hospital overheard. A body in the morgue that bears an incredible resemblance to you was also placed in there. Unfortunately for the guy, he was shot in the face. But the fingerprints will match up to what's on file."

"So it's over? I'm safe?"

"As safe as we can make you for now. Ackers's office has your information, but they don't know you're alive. No one knows you're alive but the people on this estate."

Rafe stared at Avad and then at the kids. Nola knew the news must be a shock, so she waited until he was ready to speak. Three full minutes passed. "I can't believe this."

"Ileana pulled some strings and is having new identities created for all of you. You should have them in a few days."

Rafe stared at her in shock. "How did you do this?"

"I was always planning on killing you. It was the only way to make sure that the cartel left you alone."

"And the cartel?"

"They won't care about the kids now that you're gone. They're too young to know anything. They were never the target. They were only a target because they were with you."

"So we're in the clear?"

"Looks like."

Rafe ran a hand through his hair. "What about the driver from the business park?"

"Unfortunately, he was suffocated in his hospital bed."

Rafe looked at Nola, raising an eyebrow.

She rolled her eyes. "No, I didn't suffocate him. The cartel was cleaning up their mess. They got the information from him, and then they took out the one last witness. So as far as everybody knows, you're dead."

"I don't know what to say. You planned all of this?"

"With a little help from my friends." She nodded to Avad, who stood near the kids, raking some leaves.

"I don't know what to do now."

"You don't have to make any decisions right away. And Ileana said you can stay as long as you'd like while you decide. She's also willing to offer you a job if you're interested."

Shock splashed across Rafe's face. "What?"

"Hear me out. Ileana, as you know, has been in the intelligence world for decades. She knows it better than anyone I know. Bishop will keep running security on the cartel to see if they have any inkling as to where you are so that she'll know automatically. Ileana has protection 24/7. And it's no exaggeration to say she can call in the Marines at any point if she needs them. You could live here on the estate. The kids would go to a private school only a few miles away. They would have a great education and hopefully feel safe. But most importantly, you can stay together."

Rafe stared at her, his mouth hanging open. "Why would she do this?"

Nola's gaze strayed to where Sofia and Enzo were playing. "Because you're a good family. And she likes having you around."

"*She* likes us?" Rafe asked, his voice a little deeper than it was a moment ago.

Nola stared up into his eyes and then quickly looked away, taking a step back. "We all do. You'll be safe here. You'll have a good life here."

"I can't just stay here. I have to earn my keep."

"Oh, there's always stuff to be done on the estate. Security maintenance. You any good with a hammer?"

Rafe gave her a smile. "I'm not bad."

"I'm sure Ileana will be able to come up with lots to keep you busy. And Ileana really could use an extra hand around the house. Darus's daughter just had a baby, and he wants to play grandpa a lot. But like I said, you don't have to make any decisions right away. Give yourself a couple of days to think about it."

"I don't need a couple of days. I accept. Absolutely. This is so much more than I ever imagined."

Nola smiled. "Well, then I guess you have to start imagining some more good things."

Rafe stared down at her. "I already am."

CHAPTER SIXTY-FOUR

BISHOP

BISHOP LOOKED up from her spot at the kitchen table as Ileana stepped inside. "What did she say?"

"She's going to go talk to him."

Instead of walking to join Bishop at the table, Ileana walked over to the glass, standing to the side where she had a view of Nola walking toward Rafe but where Nola would be unable to see her.

Bishop went and stood next to her. Together, they watched as Nola called Rafe over. Rafe stood so close to Nola that she needed to look up at him. And Bishop was nearly bowled over by the fact that she didn't take a step back to increase the distance.

Bishop's hopes rose. There was something there. She wasn't sure Nola would act on it or if she was even aware of it. It was obvious to anyone looking at the two of them that there was something between them.

"Do you see it?" Bishop whispered.

Sadness laced Ileana's reply. "Yes."

Bishop closed her eyes and felt like a heel. She shouldn't have said anything. After all, Nola had been married to Ileana's son. Bishop knew how much she'd loved David. *Bishop* had loved David. He was like the brother she never had.

"I'm sorry. This isn't a good idea. Maybe—"

Ileana moved next to her and took her hand in hers. "No, this is what Nola needs, and this is what David would want. For Nola to be happy. For Nola to have a home again. He wouldn't be happy knowing that his death put her on this path. He would understand it, but he would want her to find happiness again."

Bishop watched as Nola leaned toward Rafe. Bishop didn't think she even realized she was doing it. Ever since Bishop had seen Rafe and Nola together, she noticed that the two of them tended to just gravitate toward one another. It seemed like an unconscious act on both of their parts, and yet it was undeniably there.

Nola stepped away and then smiled at the kids, heading for the kitchen. Ileana quickly slipped her arm out from Bishop's and moved to the stovetop. She grabbed the kettle and started filling it with water. Bishop quickly retook her seat at the kitchen table.

Nola stepped in the door, and Bishop looked up. "Oh, hey, how'd it go?"

Nola rolled her eyes. "As if you two weren't standing at the window watching."

Bishop cringed, shooting a glance at Ileana.

"We just wanted to see how he received the idea. It looked like it went well," Ileana said.

Nola moved to the table, leaning her hands against the back of one of the chairs. "Yes. He accepted it. How long until it's finalized?"

"It usually takes two or three days. It will be done by the weekend," Ileana said.

"How long will you be staying?" Bishop asked.

"Just until the paperwork is finalized." She looked at Bishop. "Let's find me another case."

Nola strode past them and down the hall. Bishop watched her go, her heart sinking. She had really thought this time it would be different.

Ileana sat next to her at the table. "Give her time. You're not focusing on the progress. She said she'd stay for a few days. She's never done that before. So be glad. This is a good sign."

Bishop nodded with a sigh. Ileana was right.

But apparently Nola's missions weren't over just yet.

ABOUT THE AUTHOR

R.D. Brady is an American writer who grew up on Long Island, NY but has made her home in both the South and Midwest before settling in upstate New York. On her way to becoming a full-time writer, R.D. received a Ph.D. in Criminology and taught for ten years at a small liberal arts college.

R.D. left the glamorous life of grading papers behind in 2013 with the publication of her first novel, the supernatural action adventure, *The Belial Stone*. Over ten novels later and hundreds of thousands of books sold, and she hasn't looked back. Her novels tap into her criminological background, her years spent studying martial arts, and the unexplained aspects of our history. Join her on her next adventure!

To learn about her upcoming publications, sign up for her newsletter here or on her website (rdbradybooks.com).

BOOKS BY R.D. BRADY

Hominid

The Belial Series (in order)
The Belial Stone
The Belial Library
The Belial Ring
Recruit: A Belial Series Novella
The Belial Children
The Belial Origins
The Belial Search
The Belial Guard
The Belial Warrior
The Belial Plan
The Belial Witches
The Belial War
The Belial Fall
The Belial Sacrifice

The A.L.I.V.E. Series

B.E.G.I.N.
A.L.I.V.E.
D.E.A.D.
R.I.S.E.
S.A.V.E.

The Steve Kane Series

Runs Deep
Runs Deeper

The Unwelcome Series

Protect
Seek
Proxy

The Nola James Series

Surrender the Fear
Escape the Fear

Published as Riley D. Brady

The Key of Apollo
The Curse of Hecate

Be sure to sign up for R.D.'s mailing list to be the first to hear when she has a new release!

Made in the USA
Middletown, DE
18 October 2020